ODYSSEY

Stories of Journeys from around Europe from the Aarhus 39

Edited by Daniel Hahn

International Children's Literature

HAY FESTIVAL

AARHUS 39

*celebrating the best emerging writers for
young people from across wider Europe*

ALMA BOOKS LTD
3 Castle Yard
Richmond
Surrey TW10 6TF
United Kingdom
www.almabooks.com

Odyssey first published by Alma Books Ltd in 2017

Original texts © the respective authors, 2017
Translations © the respective translators, 2017
Illustrations © the respective illustrators, 2017
Full credits can be found on the Copyright Information page at the
end of the volume

Introduction © Daniel Hahn, 2017

Printed in Great Britain by CPI Group (UK) Ltd, Croydon CR0 4YY

ISBN: 978-1-84688-429-0

Contents

Introduction

On 23rd June 2016, three much loved European writers sat down for a meeting at the London offices of the Hay Festival. They had come together to select thirty-nine of the best young children's and YA writers from around Europe, the "Aarhus 39". Our three judges – Matt Haig from the UK, Kim Fupz Aakeson from Denmark and Ana Cristina Herreros from Spain – had read hundreds of pages of submissions and samples of work. They had come to the meeting equipped with notes and impressions and opinions; and over the course of a long and lively day they talked and argued and gradually made their selection. I was in the room with them, but trying extremely hard to keep my own opinions out of it. This was not easy *at all*. By the end of the day, we had a list.

There was something else happening on 23rd June 2016, too. That was the day the UK voted by a slim majority to leave the European Union. While Matt and Kim and Ana Cristina were working away at assembling their list of European writers, all around us, across the city and across the country, voters were choosing what the UK's relationship to Europe should be. About fifty-two per cent of those who voted chose to have us leave the European Union, forty-eight per cent chose to stay.

Maybe it's silly to describe these two events side by side, just because they happened to be occurring on the same date. They're altogether different kinds of event, after all. One was an intimate cultural project, and the other a vast national political and social earthquake. But I think they're connected, and I'll try and explain why.

The International Children's Literature Hay Festival in Aarhus, of which this book is a part, is about encouraging young people to read stories of other lives, other peoples' experience. It is about recognizing talent, introducing great writers and storytellers you might otherwise not have come across, from all around the continent. At its heart it's also a manifestation of our belief – all of us working on it – that stories should be allowed to move about freely. That freedom is essential to us as readers and writers, and I think we know it instinctively, even if we don't often give it much thought. Readers from over here should be able to encounter stories from over there, and vice versa; and the more we all learn to listen to each other, the better it will be for everybody.

Stories make us understand how people might be different, but also how we are all the same. As readers, we take characters who seem so very unlike us (people in other places or times, with wildly different lives, even with magical powers) and find ways of connecting to them. I can't think of anything that has the power to make that connection quite like a great work of fiction. Reading may feel like a quiet, private act, a way of isolating yourself from the world; but surrendering to a good story is also the *opposite* of isolation. It's a way of reaching out, of communicating, silently, through our powers of imagination and empathy.

The twenty-one writers in this YA collection come from fourteen different countries across Europe, and work in ten different languages. And yes, in some cases their worlds are really quite different from yours and mine. But readers in their countries are interested in stories about school, stories about relationships, about family, about sex, about arguments and reconciliations, about friendships – about all the things that make the world confusing or frightening or exhilarating. They're drawn to stories about people crossing boundaries, taking journeys, breaking rules; about young people figuring out their place in the world. So yes, maybe the stories in this collection do have their origins in Denmark or France or Russia, but they feel perfectly at home here – wherever your "here" may be.

Sitting somewhere between this book's writers and its readers, there's another group of people taking part in the conversation: the translators. They're the people who make it possible for us to read a story written in Finnish or Danish or Portuguese, even if their interference in the conversation mostly goes unnoticed. And translators, too, need to share a basic assumption: that it's possible for a story to travel great distances, shedding its original language, clothing itself in a new one, settling in a new home, and yet still have a life and something important to say. Translation depends absolutely on our having things in common. It celebrates the fact that difference exists, but recognizes that it needn't be an obstacle. And so translators are naturally generous border-crossers. The very origins of the word "translate" come from Latin: "carrying *across*".

Stories want to travel. We shouldn't expect a story to stay trapped within borders, or within languages – it's not natural, and they really don't like it. Good stories positively refuse to stay put. In this book you'll find – in English – a Spanish story set in China; a Dutch story set among the gods on Mount Olympus; a Danish story set on a refugee boat; another in Paris; a Portuguese story set... well, actually I'm not quite sure... Realistic or fantastical, light or dark, exciting or reassuring or gripping or funny – deep down these stories are all about being young, and being human. Neither of these is an easy thing to be. And honestly, what could be more interesting?

Twenty-one stories have travelled in from all around Europe to meet you, and we are proud to welcome them, all together, into this collection. We start, though, with a story from Germany, about two young friends. It has one of my favourite opening lines: *No one rings a doorbell like Pekka...*

Now, read on.

– Daniel Hahn

Odyssey

Pekka-Style

Finn-Ole Heinrich

No one rings a doorbell like Pekka. He uses the same bell as everyone else, of course, but it's louder when he rings it. It clangs more, it jangles more and it booms deep inside you. You feel it in your teeth and your bones when Pekka rings the bell – a kind of siren wail mixed with old-fangled school bell, really – it's the perfectly normal bell but different. And of course he rings until you open the door, rings and rings without mercy, Pekka-style. I slam down the stairs, leap the last landing and jerk open the gasping door. And then there he is, at the crack of dawn, ultra-relaxed, three strides away from the door – no idea how he was ringing the bell off the wall just a moment ago – sporting a cool smile like he had nothing to do with the nightmarish siren's wail, rocking back and forth on his shoes like he had half-moons on the end of his legs and not flat feet. He's tucked his thumbs behind the straps of his giant backpack like a granddad does with his braces, and he flashes me a broad grin. For at least two and three-quarter years, Pekka's been wearing these great big ancient leather shoes that look comfy as hell – no idea where he got them. He's never had another pair of shoes on since I've known him, winter or summer. Maybe he was born with them attached: they seem to be part of his body somehow.

'What's up, deadhead? Got everything?'

'Huh?'

'Kkan we go? Hurry up, you kkan chew my ear off later. Bus leaves in…' Pekka looks at his phone and raises his eyebrows. 'In nine minutes, out by the Swamp Garden.'

'What bus?'

'Henri, old fella, you pulling my leg? Did you not get my message or what?'

I think about it. Actually, yeah, I did get a message from Pekka yesterday. About nine thirty, I remember now, when I was in bed reading. To be honest, I thought he'd been pocket-dialling. What he'd sent made no sense at all. Some kind of weird number combination.

'So?' Pekka asks with a wink. And then it rains down on my head from far above – about two and a half years ago, just after he'd moved into our road, Pekka had explained his secret code to me. It had something to do with numbers and books. He'd pressed a book into my hand, one he had at home, too, the exact same edition and all that, and when he sent me numbers they stood for certain words on certain pages. No bugger could ever decode it unless he happened to know what book we used; it was a stroke of genius. Except that we'd used the secret code approximately zero times since then, because, well, to be honest no one was interested in our messages.

'Why're you standing there like a pound of sausage meat? We gotta go-ho!' Pekka points demonstratively at his non-existent watch. 'You really haven't pakked?'

I shake my head; Pekka rolls his eyes.

'Where are we going anyway?'

'You got exactly two minutes to pakk. I'll explain on the way.'

'But… and… how long will we be… on the way?'

'Get a move on! One fifty-seven!'

No idea, no idea, I think, and I run, up the stairs, down the hall, then a leap into the middle of my room. Grab my backpack and upend it: amazing things land on the floor, some of which I haven't seen for at least a year and a half – no time for that. What shall I pack?

What do you pack when you don't know what for? Sleeping bag. Trousers. Shirt. Phone, charger. Underpants, socks. Pocket knife. What else? The fake school ID card created by Pekka to make me seem sixteen. And? Half a bar of chocolate, a handful of gummy bears from my pocket, pen, toothbrush. What do I tell my parents? And how? Can't just bugger off. Write a message? No time for that. Up the hall, down the stairs. Pekka tuts when he sees me, shakes his head, sets off yelling: 'Thirty-two, it's as tight as a moskkito's arse, my friend. Put the pedal to the metal! Three and a half minutes!'

Shoes, jacket. I slam the door behind me, thinking: 'Shit, forgot the keys.' No time for that. Run after him. Pekka is running half a block ahead of me, the size of a Playmobil man. I ask myself whether fifteen seconds to tie my shoes would have been worth it over six hundred metres.

By the time we turn the corner and get a view of the Swamp Garden, the bus is just chugging off from the stop and Pekka starts yelling, jumping onto the street and waving his arms like a shipwrecked man on an island when a boat floats past a hundred miles away. But of course the bus just goes chugging on, doesn't matter what kind of circus you put on: bus drivers never stop for you when you turn up late and still want to get on, you can shout and wail as much as you like. Everyone knows that. Not even if they stop at the lights and only have to open the door. Never. Old bus drivers' rule.

Pekka is rooted to the spot in the middle of the crossroads, looking around. Cars drive towards him, then around him, hooting, braking, jostling. Pekka stands there and thinks. He stares at me, and I can tell he's thinking, because his eyebrows are drawn together into a single crossbar, like someone had underlined his forehead with a Sharpie. Suddenly he turns round and looks somewhere else; I look down at my untied laces and wonder whether it was really my fault. After three or four seconds, Pekka turns back to me and waves me over with a sweep of the arm. What am I supposed to do in the middle of the crossroads? I look for a gap in the traffic and fight a slow way through to him. By the time I get there he tuts and grouches: 'About time!' So here we are, in amidst the cars' blasting.

And now?

'Takksi, you reptile. You lookk in that direkktion, I'll takke this one. When one comes, don't wave it down – jump in front of it.'

'That's really dangerous.'

'Mmh, yeah. That direkktion!' says Pekka strictly, pointing mine out again. Just as I'm about to turn around I see him leaping from the central strip onto the carriageway with arms outstretched. Screeching tyres—

'Listen mate,' says the moustachioed taxi driver, a man with a smell of tobacco, coffee, car freshener and recently wiped-down fake leather. We're on the back seat, our backpacks between us. All I can see of Pekka is his hands and legs.

'You can't just hop right in front of my vehicle, you get me? It's bloody dangerous. I'm doing seventy along here – you know my braking distance?'

'You're only allowed to do fifty here,' is Pekka's growled response. 'We need to get to the station, quick. Do seventy if you like.'

The taxi driver makes an astounding sound from somewhere inside his head, like behind his nose, behind his mouth, between throat and brain, sort of heading downwards. It sounds like some kind of inner toilet flush, a rolling gurgle intended to express his lack of approval and at the same time wash all disapproving thoughts down into his beer belly.

There's a moment of silence; I stare out of the window.

'Pekka,' I say after a while.

Mh, Pekka grunts, still angry because we missed the bus, because I hadn't packed, because I hadn't deciphered his message.

'Where are we going, anyway?'

'The bus station, you softball.' And at that instant the taxi driver is pulling in and I look at the meter and it says 12.80, and I look over at Pekka because I haven't even thought of that: bringing money. Mind you, I wouldn't have had any anyway, maybe two euros and a few coppers. I look at Pekka's scabbed knee and hear him rummaging in his backpack, and then I see his hands and in them a plastic bag from a supermarket, which he opens, and in the bag I see a shedload of money – don't know how much exactly, but it must be… a thousand euro or something, a whole lot, all these notes, grey, red, blue, brown, even green ones I think. It's incredible. Where did Pekka get all that cash from and why has he brought so much money along in the first place? What do we need it for? What the hell's he planning this time? You never know with Pekka. All his crazy ideas and notions… Does he want to go somewhere and buy special frog spawn at a discount price like last spring, or pick up really good kefir grains, a hundred pairs of trainers or a couple of strap-on sausage grills? I'm sure it'll only be two or three years before Pekka's a millionaire or behind bars. Probably both. And happy as Larry.

I've never been to the bus station. It's pretty much like the normal station, just a bit scruffier. It smells like the morning after a big street party. There are people everywhere, perched on top of huge bags, with vacant eyes and faces like they've been absent-mindedly modelled out of mincemeat. Some of them are digging in the bins, and when a bus comes and spits people out they bugger off as fast as they can. Pekka drags me over to Bay Nine. I look at the display: Frankfurt.

'Frankfurt?'

Pekka nods.

'We're going to Frankfurt? What do we want there? Can we just do this? I have to call my…'

But Pekka's off again. A neon-green man opens the luggage compartment in the belly of the bus and Pekka throws his huge backpack inside. He looks around and assumes I'll just do exactly the same as him. Yeah, well. That's what happens. That's what I've been doing for the past three years, nearly. Pekka joins the queue for the bus door and gives a scarecrow of a guy a tap on the shoulder. The old dude turns around beneath his cap, looks down at Pekka and immediately flashes a gigantic smile. He has a pretty interesting collection of dental remains to display, and you can tell by the way his face is only partly shaved that he must have neglected a few regions of his head over the past couple of years.

'My name's Pekka,' says Pekka, holding a hand out to the old dude.

'Juppi,' says the old dude, takes Pekka's hand and operates it like a car jack, up-down-up-down.

'My best buddy,' says Pekka with a nod to me – 'Henri.'

'Hello Henri,' says Juppi and up-downs my arm like he's got two pots of coffee inside him.

'Juppi,' says Pekka, 'so you're heading for Frankkfurt too?'

'Sure thing.'

'Nice one. Awesome city,' says Pekka, and Juppi shrugs. 'Are you from Frankkfurt?'

'No. Or yeah,' says Juppi. He shrugs again. 'Who knows,' he says with a grin. 'You know, I'm living a bit between places right now,' he whispers, and giggles like a little kid.

'Tickets,' says the neon-green man, and Juppi turns round and retrieves a crumpled piece of paper from his pocket. While neon man is waiting, Pekka starts waving our tickets around behind Juppi, gesturing to neon man that we're with Juppi and Juppi's a wee bit on the confused side and it might take a minute, at which neon man gives us a relaxed nod. 'Pekka, you sly fox,' I think. Neon man scans Juppi's ticket and our tickets and on we get, no problem. Juppi starts singing the moment we board the bus and Pekka looks at me, rolling his eyes. When Juppi sits down, Pekka keeps walking, pats him on the shoulder and flops onto a seat a few rows behind him. Pekka takes a loud breath.

'Made it, dude.'

I sit down next to him.

'Erm,' I go. But Pekka cuts me off with a closing hand. That means: say nothing. I say nothing. The neon doors close. The engine starts up. Juppi's still warbling away in front of us, full of the joys of spring. The bus pulls out. We really are going to Frankfurt. We're taking a bus to another town. Which is pretty much certainly totally *verboten*. Which is absolutely…

'Hey, Pekka,' I say.

'WHAT?'

'Are we really going to Frankfurt?'

'Dude! Yes. Go and ask the bus driver if you like.'

'And what are we going to do there?'

Pekka grins and says nothing at all. Just grins. Helluva long.

'I can't just go to some random place! When will we get back? My parents will flip out. It's so totally *verboten*. I'll be grounded till Christmas.'

'Fiddlestikks. We're taking a vakkation. You just give them a quikk kkall and explain it all to your loving mummy. That's the plan.'

'What am I… How am I supposed to explain it?'

'You messed it up with the message, but it was all planned ages ago and you definitely totally told her before and she's just forgotten and so on and I'd bookked the tikkets ages ago what with you know and they'd have gone to waste and all that and you know the skkore and so on.'

'That'll never work, never.'

'Sure it will.'

'What are we doing in Frankfurt?'

'It's the skkool holidays, Henri Baby, and we're taking a vakkation. To see my father. I'm inviting you along. And tell Mummy we'll send her a postkkard and a thousand kkissy-kkisses.'

ez, Pekka, I… it's… Oh, Jesus.'

'Don't lose your kkool, it's fine, we're not kkids any more.'

'What are we then?'

'For Pete's sakke, I'm almost ten and you're over eleven – if you add us together we were grown up last year, almost. We've got everything under kkontrol.'

Pekka is the craziest nine-year-old I know. I wouldn't normally hang out with nine-year-olds, obviously, being eleven and a third myself, but Pekka's not a normal guy, he's not a nine-year-old whining baby. He usually acts like a grown-up, just one that the grown-ups' rules don't apply to yet. I mean, the rules that let you do things do apply because he'll soon be grown up anyway, but as long as he's still a kid he makes the most of the advantages of being a kid as well. There aren't that many advantages, but there are a few. Sometimes you get in places cheaper, most people turn a blind eye and if you act cute they'll even help you out. You can get away with all kinds of crap and they won't put you in jail. And another thing: you can earn as much cash as you want and you don't have to pay any taxes. Pekka explained it once, but I didn't really get it. It's like, when you earn two euros when you're grown up, you have to pay one euro in taxes, to the state or whatever and they use it to build roads and schools. But kids? Zero. Because they think kids don't earn anything anyway. That's why Pekka wants to earn all the money he'll need in life by the time he's fifteen and then retire. He'll be a man of independent means – that's what they call it. He's got five and a half years to go, and you can bet he'll make it. I'll probably join in.

With a hydraulic sigh, the bus's neon-green belly flap opens up and reveals the bags and cases, shaken and shuffled like building blocks in a box. Pekka drags his backpack out of the tangle. We wave goodbye to Juppi and then head through the crowds at Frankfurt bus station and straight down to an underground platform. I do feel kind of funny here, on our own like this, not knowing my way around and all that, but Pekka forges impeccably ahead and knows exactly what to do. Knows where we have to go, how to get there, where everything is and where we are. We find a ticket machine and Pekka taps at the screen.

'Have you been here before?' I ask.

'Nope.'

'So how do you know—'

'Dude: research! Here' – he pulls his hand out of his pocket and drops a jangling load of coins in my hand. 'Pay the money.'

We get on a train and zoom around the huge-looking city. Pekka produces sandwiches and a thermos flask of coffee from his backpack. He's the only person under sixteen I know who really likes drinking coffee. He hands me a cup and an excellent sandwich. We chew away and I force down his bitter black coffee: apparently it makes your man hair grow faster – on your chin and chest and balls I mean. Pekka grunts quietly and chews, with a satisfied grin on his face.

Translated from the German by Katy Derbyshire

Illustrated by Satoshi Kitamura

Andy and the Puppies

Stefanie de Velasco

Don't let him off the leash, I hear Mama's voice say, echoing in my ears, distant, as if between me and the world outside is a wall, a wall of ice, though there's no ice in my ears, how could there be, and it's not Mama next to me, it's Aylin. We just wanted to stop briefly in Hasenheide park, let Spartacus run around a little, and now this. Don't let him off the leash, Mama said, do you hear me? Mama always says that, but I always let Spartacus off the leash anyway, just like everyone else does in Hasenheide.

We'd nearly made it to the dog run when this female dog in heat suddenly showed up. She was ugly, but Spartacus doesn't care about looks as long as they're in heat. It happened really quickly, they played with each other for only a few seconds before he mounted her. Aylin and I tried to run down into the hollow to try to separate them, but it was all snowed in and slippery. Aylin and I screamed at them, we threw the leash at Spartacus as well as our Nike duffel bag, Aylin even threw her water bottle, but Spartacus didn't care, nothing was going to disturb him.

I looked around for an owner, but there was nobody there. I thought, OK, good, I don't have to say anything to Mama if Spartacus gets a stray dog pregnant, I thought, but then somebody showed up. He came running out of the rhododendrons, a man, well over six feet tall, dressed from head to toe in black leather, with his head shaved and a giant white butterfly tattooed on it.

Maja, the man called when he saw what was happening in the hollow in front of the dog run, but just like us he slipped in the snow, and just like us he threw all sorts of things at Maja, an e-cigarette, the chain attached to his wallet, and something else that looked like pepper spray, but it didn't do any good either.

Now Aylin and I are standing next to the man, and all three of us are looking down at Spartacus and Maja. Spartacus climbs off of Maja. They're both finished, but something seems to be wrong. Their hindquarters are stuck to each other, I know it sounds crazy, but that's exactly what it is. Maja and Spartacus can't pull apart. I'm about to go down but the man with the butterfly tattoo on his head holds me back.

Too late, he says, they're already stuck.

Aylin and I look at each other.

What do you mean, stuck?

The man sighs and pulls a cigarette out of his leather jacket. It's much bigger and fatter than a normal cigarette and when he lights it the smoke smells sweet.

Dogs get stuck together, says the man, that's the way nature made them, to make sure it works. Dogs don't take any chances when it comes to fucking.

Aylin blushes. We've never heard anyone say fucking before.

We can't separate them now, says the man, it could injure them. Which one of you owns the dog?

I slowly raise my hand, like in school, and I can feel my lower lip start to tremble, and a second later big teardrops are running down my cheeks, they're super hot, because when it comes out that Spartacus has gotten a dog pregnant there will be serious trouble at home.

It's not so bad, says the man pulling a crumpled packet of tissues out of his jacket, I'm Andy, he says, but then he asks for my number because you have to. The owner of the male dog is liable to the owner of the female dog. It's nerve-wracking and costs money, and I don't have any money, so Mama can't find out, no way, otherwise she won't let me go to Greece during summer break and she'll take away my allowance.

Maybe it didn't work, says this Andy guy.

After a while, Spartacus and Maja are apparently no longer stuck together. They bark and come running up to us, they look really happy, their mouths are open as if they are smiling.

I won't say see you soon, says Andy putting on Maja's leash, but if something happens I'll call you.

At home I go online and google everything about puppies and birth and pregnancy. It takes about two months in a mother's belly for a puppy to be finished. On Youtube, a dog giving birth looks like something totally normal. The mother lays in a basket and squirms around. Once in a while she stands up and when she does a pup slides out of her wrapped in a bubble of slime. She licks it off and the pup starts to breathe. It's messy, there's a lot of blood, but it's also somehow beautiful. For the first few weeks the mother does everything for the pups. She even eats their poop, it's something normal in the wild, because of predators, and it's not poisonous.

I don't hear anything from Andy for months. Once in a while I see him with Maja at Hasenheide, but I always hide. At first Maja looks normal, but then she starts to get heavier. Maybe he won't get in touch at all, I hope, maybe he feels sorry for me, a girl who didn't pay attention well enough, maybe he forgot, but Andy hadn't forgotten me. One night I get a text: *Congratulations. Spartacus just became a father*. I lie awake for the rest of the night. But I don't text back. I know I'm being shameful, like our friend Carla's father. Alimony, that's what it's called, he's supposed to pay it, but he doesn't. He doesn't take responsibility, that's what Mama always says, that's the type of person I am now, but I don't care, I can even feel for all those fathers. You don't want to think about it, you just hope the other person forgets you, it must feel the same to them. Everything goes fine for two weeks, the Andy guy doesn't try to get in touch, but then I get another text, at school, during a morning break: *Some bad news to go with the good news. I have to go to jail for 30 days. Meet at 3 at the dog run, Andy*.

Aylin covers her face with her hands, and I nearly drop my phone in shock.

That's it, says Aylin, you have to talk to your mom now.

And have her find out and have my trip to Greece cancelled? No way.

But you can't meet someone who's going to jail!

I won't, I say, we will.

We go to the dog run with Spartacus in the afternoon. We recognize Andy's tattooed head from far away.

You have to come to my place, he says when he's standing in front of us, Maja can't be away from the puppies for long.

No problem, I say even though I'm really scared. I have to literally pull Aylin along with me. We reach the edge of Hasenheide and head along Fontanestraße. Andy stops in front of a building at the end of the block and unlocks the door. The mailboxes are all broken. There are heaps of garbage in the courtyard. It stinks of cold cigarettes and diapers. Andy trudges into a stairwell off the courtyard, and up to the top floor.

Aylin's hand is soaked with sweat.

What if he kidnaps us, Aylin whispers in my ear, locks us in and never lets us out again, like that girl in Austria, but I hold her hand even more tightly so she can't run off. Andy opens the apartment door. We look around in silence. We've never seen a place like this in our entire lives. I'm not even sure you can even call it a place of residence. The word residence comes from reside, I always thought, but nobody would want to reside here. The kitchen is full of broken appliances and so filthy that someone has nailed two boards across the doorway to keep people out. Next to the kitchen is a large room, but there's nothing in it but an empty cabinet and over by the window an old sofa with a sleeping bag on it.

Sorry, says Andy slumping down on the sofa, I'm broke at the moment. I had to sell everything, the last things to go were my model cars that were in the cabinet.

Maja walks to the back corner of the room. You can hear soft squeals. Six little puppies are lying back there on a dirty, blood-smeared blanket. They are all different colours, white, brown, black, spotted. Maja has barely laid down before the pups are hanging from her swollen red teats, suckling. Spartacus goes over to his children, but he just sniffs at them for a second and then comes back to us. Maja looks a bit pissed off. She reminds me of someone. Oh right, Mama, when I don't want to eat breakfast, or she has to look at something from school and sign it. I bet she'd rather be running around the park playing go-fetch.

How cute, says Aylin squatting next to the blanket and putting on her lap a brown puppy that looks like Spartacus as a baby. Its eyes are blue. Andy grabs the biggest pup and pets him. I want to keep this one, he says, but it probably won't work.

Why, I ask.

Andy sighs.

I fucked up. I'm not proud of it. I was in the slammer for a long time. You know, jail.

Is that where that's from, asks Aylin pointing to the butterfly.

Andy nods.

I haven't been out that long, couple of years. I have to make a payment every month, to pay off the fine, but I lost my job at the slaughterhouse because of Maja and the puppies. I was late to work twice and they fired me. I can't make my payment, so I have to go back to prison. Either you pay or you get locked up.

How much money do you need, I ask.

Andy looks at us.

A lot of money. Five hundred euros. You don't have that kind of money, right?

I have fifty, I say, in my piggy bank.

Me too, says Aylin.

Well, says Andy, I have a hundred, too, which makes two hundred. Maybe that will appease the court cashier.

What's that, the court cashier?

It's the government payment office. Where you pay fines.

Aha, says Aylin looking at Andy.

Can I ask you something, she says.

Spit it out, says Andy.

Why were you in prison?

Andy gulps.

Behind his back I make an are-you-crazy hand signal, as in, you don't ask somebody that, but Aylin doesn't look at me, she just keeps looking at Andy.

Grievous bodily harm, says Andy.

Aylin turns white. So do I. I can feel all the blood draining out of my head like it's running out a faucet somebody turned on all the way.

I didn't mean to, says Andy, I just wanted to give him a good punch. It was at my old job. There was a young kid. And one of my coworkers was constantly tormenting him. And then one time I saw the guy stuff the kid into a locker. I flipped out. The poor kid, he was mentally retarded.

You can't say retarded, says Aylin.

OK, handicapped, says Andy.

You don't say that either.

What do you say, asks Andy looking at Aylin.

He has a developmental disability, says Aylin, like my brother.

Okay, he had a developmental disability, says Andy, in any event I flipped out. I didn't just punch the guy, I kept punching him. You ever heard of David and Goliath?

Only the names, I say.

One hit to the wrong spot and you die straight away. It was a question of a few centimetres, says Andy taking a second puppy onto his lap.

For a while he just pets the pup, and nobody says a word.

Animals are better than people. People are monsters, you'll learn that one day, says Andy placing the whimpering puppies back on Maja's teats, you should go home. I don't need your money. I have nobody to blame but myself. Go home, it's fine.

Aylin and I look at each other.

The next day we meet at my place. We have a plan.

We break open our piggy banks and put all the money in an envelope. I creep to the countertop in the kitchen and grab the jar full of two-euro coins that Mama keeps hidden behind the food dehydrator. I take out ten coins, then we go to the store and buy dog food and meatballs, rolls and mustard, and then carry it all to Andy's, all the way upstairs, all by ourselves.

Andy opens the door. He is holding another one of the big, sweet cigarettes. When he sees us with all the bags, he gets quiet.

Give this to the court cashier, says Aylin handing him the envelope with a hundred euros, you need to stay with Maja.

Thanks, stammers Andy.

Aylin and I have to smile. It's fun to see how happy Andy is. We sit down with the puppies, Andy eats his meatballs and Spartacus acts like an idiot. He shows no interest whatsoever in his children, he's only interested in Andy's meatballs, and when one of the pups runs up to him and nips him playfully on the paw, Spartacus growls at him.

Stop it, I yell grabbing his collar.

That's how dogs are as fathers, says Andy, and some people, too. Mine was no different.

Not mine, says Aylin, mine is nice. And funny!

Little dogs only need their mother, says Andy.

Yeah, says Aylin, but it's different with people. We need a father, and not just boys. Girls too.

Of course, says Andy, we're people, not animals.

What are you going to do with the puppies when they get bigger, I ask.

Andy clears his throat.

You'll have to help me with that. They have to be immunized. Then I'll put up a sign and we'll find good homes for them, what do you think?

As long as my mother doesn't catch wind of it, I say and then I tell Andy the story about the leash and the trip to Greece. Andy listens to me, he doesn't laugh like Uncle Fitzi does sometimes, he really understands that the whole thing with Mama and Spartacus could be a big problem for me.

Don't worry, he says, I'll figure it out. I start a new job on Monday, at a different slaughterhouse.

No, says Aylin, we want to help.

And we do. Aylin and I do something that we've wanted to do for a long time, because now we have a good reason to. Every Saturday we meet at Alexanderplatz, Aylin with her guitar and me with my flute. We put the guitar case in front of us and play classics. The coins rain down. Two girls making music on the street make way more money than a Russian concert master , it's not fair, but right now I'm glad for it. We go to Alexanderplatz every Saturday and then afterwards we go with Spartacus through Hasenheide to Andy's, stopping beforehand to buy meatballs. We give Andy our money, and he buys dog food with it and saves up the rest for the immunizations.

The puppies keep getting bigger and stronger. At some point Maja starts to get annoyed and nips at them when they try to suckle, she wants her peace and quiet.

I was at the vet yesterday, says Andy biting into a meatball on a roll, we'll immunize the puppies next week, and people are coming to look at them starting tomorrow.

Aylin sits down next to Maja and cuddles the puppies. We'd prefer to keep them all, but it won't work.

I think when this is over, says Andy, I'll have Maja spayed.

Spayed?

Andy runs his hand over his shaved head, it looks like he's petting the butterfly's wings.

I mean have her sterilized, remove the cervix and all that. They take it all out, he says.

Aylin grimaces like she has a toothache.

I look at my watch.

We have to go. Let us know if you need any more help, but Andy shakes his head.

I can manage it by myself from here on out, he says shaking our hands ceremoniously.

You've become good fathers, says Andy smiling at us.

On our way home through Hasenheide, Aylin suddenly stops.

Do we have a cervix too, she asks.

Of course, I say, don't you remember those shots a few months ago?

Oh right, says Aylin, against cervical cancer.

Exactly, I say.

Can you have your cervix removed?

Honestly, says Aylin, when I grow up and have children of my own, I really will be a good father, not one like Spartacus, one who takes just as much care as we do. Otherwise I'll do that too.

Do what?

Have my cervix removed, says Aylin.

Translated from the German by Tim Mohr

When I Open My Eyes the World's Askew

Annette Münch

We walk towards a bench in the middle of a small patch of grass behind a boarded-up kiosk. Green bushes and trees screen the park from the roads around it, where cars sit in queues. The boys hanging out by the bench smile and greet Theo. Firm handshakes and slaps on shoulders and *'sup bro* in loud voices. And me in the background, my heart pounding, my armpits already damp. I long to be back in my uncle and aunt's flat, back in their guest bed in that quiet room with the door that I can close.

All the others are wearing trainers and hoodies with big logos. My T-shirt is grey and drab like the morning fog. It hangs loosely on my body, which has waved goodbye to several kilos in the last year. It's cold for August, too, and the skin on my arms breaks out into goosebumps. No doubt the boys can see it and think I'm a loser.

'This is my cousin, Simon. The one visiting from the south,' Theo explains. 'This is Mathis, Leon and Bilal.'

The boys stare at me and my instinct tells me to run.

'You're from Kristiansand, right?' asks the one who called Theo 'bro'. His ears stick out like two handles from under his cap. I nod.

'And you came all the way here to stay with this sweaty loser?' says another, laughing and gesturing at Theo, who pretends he's offended and whacks his hand away. 'I'm Mathis, by the way. My granddad was from just outside Kristiansand. He used to hunt and stuff.'

'I'm taking my hunting-licence exam next year,' I mumble, too quietly. 'I got it for my sixteenth birthday, so I'd get out more.'

All the muscles in my body tense as everyone turns to look at me. *We often interpret facial expressions negatively*, my psychologist once said. Then she and I had looked at pictures of facial expressions in a folder and discussed how they weren't necessarily negative after all.

I try to take deep breaths.

'Cool,' says the one who called Theo 'bro'. 'So you can shoot a rifle?'

I nod and look down at my new, whiter-than-white shoes.

'Then you can shoot bears and elk. And buy guns legally!' Mathis interjects. 'We scared some guys with an airsoft gun a while back. They thought it was real and scattered!'

Everyone laughs and I find myself smiling too. I straighten up, wipe the palms of my hands on my trousers and decide not to tell them I probably won't be felling bears just yet.

'Could you take the exam with him?' Mathis asks Theo.

My cousin hesitates: 'Nah, don't got time.'

Mathis proffers a lopsided grin.

'Bullshit, it's cos you got the aim of a half-blind old lady!'

He turns to me: 'Last weekend he tried to kick a guy who was making trouble, but he missed and hit a bin. He could barely walk home!'

Everyone bursts out laughing, except Theo. He just runs a hand over his brown-black hair, which is stiff with wax. I smile. Not because the story's funny, but because it feels good to be part of a group, chatting and joking around again. Theo lights a joint and takes a puff before passing it to Mathis, who inhales and slowly blows smoke rings. The smell of the weed smarts in my nostrils.

'Want some?' Theo asks.

'No, thanks.'

My voice is louder now, but my mouth is still dry as an autumn leaf.

'Sensible,' says the one who called Theo 'bro', grinning. 'And to think you're related to Theo!'

Theo snorts as Mathis and Bilal laugh and each take another puff.

'It's cool you came out tonight,' Theo says suddenly. 'After being home so long. Did the psychologist use to come to you?'

The silence is deafening. Everyone's looking at me again. I feel my anxiety surface like a bear from hibernation.

'My cousin has mental-health problems,' Bilal says. 'The doctor prescribes pills and she gives them to me. You got any extra?'

I stammer when I say yes, I think so. Without thinking, I shove my hand in my trouser pocket and pull out the almost empty blister pack I brought just to tide me over. Bilal takes it, looking pleased.

'I have a lot more at home,' I say, relieved. 'At one point I had so many prescriptions my room looked like a pharmacy.'

The boys grin and say that that must have been awesome and that I'll have to bring more next time. I meet Theo's eyes, but can't work out how he's feeling.

'You're such an addict, Bilal,' Mathis says.

Bilal just laughs and says you can't be an addict if smoking one joint sends you to sleep. Then everyone starts discussing who's addicted to what. They're talking about things I haven't heard of, so I just laugh when they laugh and shake my head when they shake their heads, and think this might be the best evening I've had in ages.

Then Theo's mobile rings. He brings it to his ear and covers the other with his palm.

'Dasher wants us to come,' he says after hanging up. 'Now.'

Soon afterwards two dark BMWs and an Audi turn up to collect us. Mathis gets into the back seat of the one at the front and shouts over to me.

'In here, Simon!'

Every cell in my body resists as I force my legs to walk towards the door. I end up sitting in the middle, sandwiched so tightly between Mathis and Theo that they must be able to smell my sweat. No doubt they regret bringing me along. The driver's face is hidden under a cap. All I can see is something shining in his ear and a dark, snake-shaped tattoo coming out from under his neckband. The car accelerates and I'm pressed back into the leather seat. I don't know where we're going and don't think Theo knows either. My chest tightens.

Hip-hop pumps out of the speakers while we head out of town.

'I expect you could do with a bit of excitement!' Theo says, smiling. I'm suddenly unsure what a smile like that really means.

Mumbling, I ask where we're going.

'Dasher and his gang are all about cash and hot girls,' Mathis says. 'You'd have to be mad not to be friends with them.'

Shop windows, neon signs and colourful logos blur together outside.

'The police called us a gang not that long ago,' Theo says with poorly concealed pride in his voice. 'In the paper. They said we're part of "a gang environment that has emerged in the last year".'

A horn cuts through the air and a blue tram grazes the car bonnet. The driver slams on the brakes so we're thrown forward and back in our seats, and he yells 'Motherfucker!'

Minutes later we swerve out onto the motorway.

The cars stop on the forecourt outside a shopping centre. The sky is full of grey clouds that look like dirty cotton wool, and the chaotic soundscape of the city centre is gone. A forested ridge sticks up from behind the building, and on the other side of the car park there is a lone petrol station. I scramble out of the car and take a deep breath of the fresh evening air. Before Theo, Mathis, Bilal and Leon have got out, even more people appear. I try to hide behind my cousin. A couple of the boys look older, perhaps in their twenties. I glance around and see shaved heads and the contours of huge muscles through tight T-shirts. A guy with scars that look like claw marks left by a wild animal on his right cheek speaks to Theo in a language

I don't understand. Then the older boys start to leave. Their faces are impassive – they remind me of the toy soldiers I had as a child.

'Come on,' Theo says, starting to follow the others towards the entrance.

My breathing hitches. All the muscles in my body have started to tense up.

'You scared?' he asks, grinning.

His friends have almost reached the entrance. I look down at the ground. My legs are frozen, and something in my brain backfires just at the thought of being in an unknown, busy building with loads of strangers.

In the end Theo gives up and goes on without me. Perhaps he saw the tears in the corners of my eyes.

'Wait out here, then!' he shouts.

I watch his back as the sliding doors close behind him. And then I stand there. In the middle of a big open space somewhere outside of town. People with bags in their hands hurry past, car locks beep and a woman leans against a brick wall, laughing loudly on her mobile. My anxiety rears its ugly head. I know she's laughing at me.

Then five boys come round the corner. Their faces are set, and they're all holding long, dark objects. They disappear through the sliding doors before I get a closer look. A loud car horn makes me

jump. I realize I'm standing in the middle of a shopping-centre forecourt and an irritated guy in a Peugeot is trying to get past.

First a deep voice shouts, then there are angry yells and protests. Then I hear a loud bang. Someone screams. Two women and a group of small children are the first to come running through the sliding doors. Through the opening I see clusters of people barging into each other, a chaos of bodies and kicking legs, and arms and fists, and faces hidden by grey hoods. The sliding doors slowly close again. I hear glass breaking. The sliding doors open and several people run outside. Two uniformed security guards appear. I stand and stare as my skin prickles and my mouth gets drier. My T-shirt is plastered to my sweaty skin, even though I feel ice-cold.

Try to work out where the bad feelings are in your body, my psychologist once said.

But right now I can't do anything but stand immobile and let those feelings overwhelm me.

The sliding doors open again. Among the people storming out I see Theo's surprised face. He's headed for the exit at full speed. Our eyes meet and he opens his mouth as if to shout something. Then an arm comes at him from the side. The movement is lightning fast. I don't see the blow land, just Theo continuing on for a few metres before stumbling and falling to his knees. The guy that hit him disappears into the chaos. Another loud bang. People leap over Theo to get outside. Someone steps on him. It feels as if a clammy hand is trying to break my heart into a million pieces. I hear quick footsteps against the ground all around me. My instinct tells me to run, and this time I listen. My body twitches and now my legs are ready to go. I throw one last look at the shopping centre and see Theo lying on the floor with his face twisted in pain. When our eyes meet again, I see the fear in his eyes.

I run as fast as I can. Not away from the centre, but towards the entrance. Towards the darkness between the shopping centre's gaping jaws, where Theo hasn't moved an inch. A man in a suit on his way out at full speed pushes me aside and I almost fall on my face.

'Idiot!' he shouts.

I hurry on through the sliding doors. The blood roars in my ears and the nauseating taste of iron floods my mouth.

'We have to go!' I say, leaning over Theo, out of breath.

'Can't… move…' he murmurs.

He's lying curled up on the tiles and he stares at me, his pupils blown. His skin is grey and clammy.

'Are you listening? We have to go!' I say again.

Theo doesn't answer, his expression somewhat distant. He looks at me as if I'm speaking a foreign language.

I don't know what to do. I know Theo will never forgive me if I call his parents.

'Come on!' I say.

Theo looks past me in confusion. In the end I crouch down, put his arm around my shoulders and lift him up. I don't know where I get the strength. Everything is swirling around me, like I'm in a hurricane.

I fix my eyes on the exit, and haul Theo after me.

The summer air hits me in the face as the sliding doors open in front of us. Out on the forecourt some of the black cars have already gone. I see Mathis throw himself into the back seat of one of the BMWs. He's about to slam the door closed when I shout.

'Wait for us!'

Mathis looks around inside the car and then back at me. His eyes are huge and dark. The sound of sirens cuts through the evening air.

'Theo's hurt!' I add, as if the sight of us isn't explanation enough.

We're perhaps ten metres away when Mathis shouts back.

'There's no more room!'

Then he closes the door and the car screams off the forecourt.

I don't know where to take Theo, so I set him down on the ground. His eyes have started to look more alive again now. He grimaces as he presses the palms of his hands against the asphalt and carefully lies himself down. Then he just lies there, breathing shallowly through clenched teeth. A woman carrying a howling little girl jogs past.

'It's all right,' I pant.

I kneel next to Theo and support his neck with my hand. His face has regained a touch of its normal colour now.

People swarm around us. I turn and see several people filming on their mobiles.

The sirens get louder.

'Simon?' Theo groans.

His knee seems to be locked at an unnatural angle.

'Yes?' I ask.

Then there are heavy footsteps. Shadows fall across the ground before us.

I feel a hand on my shoulder. My arm is wrenched behind my back and intense pain shoots through my head. My cheek is pressed against the cold asphalt as the reverberation from the bang gradually fades in my ears. When I open my eyes the world's askew. I see black shoes and a woman in a red and neon-yellow uniform bending over Theo. Pain radiates faintly from my ribs, which are pressed against the ground.

'I've not done anything!' I try to tell them.

It feels as if my shoulders are about to dislocate. I groan in pain. Small stones press into my cheek. Something thin and hard is put around my wrists. A knee presses down on my back, making it difficult to breathe.

In the background I see Theo being lifted onto a stretcher. The cold sweat eases and my heart stops pounding. My anxiety dissipates. As I lie there and wait, the smell of dry dust in my nostrils, my head clears, until it's quiet as the heart of a deep forest. I'm not afraid of what will happen. As they take me away, I actually feel just a little bit lighter than I did before.

Translated from the Norwegian by Siân Mackie

Illustrations by Søren Jessen

We're Practising to Be Grown-ups

Peder Frederik Jensen

Mussa lowered his head to his chest and I flicked him on the bridge of his nose.

Idiot, he said.

We were sitting in a large sewer pipe behind the school. Mussa had his backpack with him.

Listen, do you get cold a lot? I asked.

Why?

Because you're not from Denmark. Because you—

Because I'm from Africa? he interrupted.

Because you're... from down there.

Tim, you're an idiot.

I dug out a lump of hash from my pocket. I rolled it in my fingers a few times.

What? Mussa looked at me. I felt his gaze on me, and his white teeth appeared when he turned his head towards the opening of the pipe.

Nothing, I said, and handed him the lump. Check out how sticky it is from all the THC.

Alhamdulillah, Mussa said, with a laugh.

I undid my jacket to roast a cigarette in the shelter of the flap. I crumbled the hash onto my palm. It stuck to my fingertips. I rubbed off the remaining pieces.

The opening of the sewer pipe must have looked like a dark eye from a distance. Sparks from the lighter, the eye of a dragon.

He had rung me two hours earlier. Said that he had to stop by. That I had to help him. A little later he stood in front of my block of flats carrying a bag.

I'm scared, he said a few minutes later when he'd made it upstairs.

Of what? I asked.

He held out his hands.

The blood clung to his nails in black ridges, to his lifeline like a dark river.

The hall in my mum's flat is narrow. White runners line the floor, there's a mirror with a pink plastic frame. There is a door to the kitchen, one to the living room – where she also sleeps – one to my room and one to the bathroom. It was like it was closing in on us: the narrow passage between the front door and the rooms of the flat grew cramped, as if we were being pushed a little closer to each other, closer to what we had so often spoken of: revenge.

Mussa washed his hands under the running water. He opened his bag and showed me the knife.

Don't touch it, he said.

It was covered in dried blood.

Why didn't you toss it? I asked.

I don't know anything, Mussa replied. All I know is I have to get away from here. I have to get out of the country. If nothing else, I have to go to Somalia.

I turned off the water. He wiped his hands on a towel.

Mussa, dammit, I said.

He's dead, he answered.

…

Are you crying?

We went into the kitchen. He sat down on a stool and started to shake. He was shaking so badly that the three thin chair legs began to clatter against the linoleum. He kept looking at his hands, rubbing his palms together, stretching his fingers. He got up and sat down again, unable to keep still.

I gave him a glass of water. I thought that in a normal family a teenager would just be able to ring his parents; they would come home, they would contact the police and Mussa would be led away in a sea of blinking blue lights. The next day and the day after that, I would visit him at a young offenders' institution, where most people would be dark-skinned like him, where he would be treated as riff-raff, labelled and put in a box – violence, foreigners, that whole thing.

Instead I sat down and said: Mussa. Relax. Drink some water. Have a cigarette. Remember what he did to your mum, to you. Remember how he beat you. How often you told me about it. Remember that, Mussa. All we have is each other. I'll help you, do you understand?

He settled down and lit one of my mum's rollies. I rolled a joint. We smoked it. It helped.

Mussa, I said, and he looked at me. I stretched out my hand and touched his clean-shaven head.

You've done the world a favour.

I found the pills that my mum normally takes when she is all wound up. Normally after one of the older, well-dressed men had removed their coat from the hook in the hall, had combed their hair in the mirror, sized themselves up from the side, laced their expensive shoes and caught the steps one by one down the flight of stairs, before disappearing in an Audi, a Volvo, an Alfa Romeo. I gave him one and it was like his cheeks went completely flaccid, like his brain collapsed into apathetic calm.

For the next couple of hours he just lay motionless on the sofa. I walked round the flat. Looked outside. In the small gardens lining the row of terraced houses, the world repeated itself with minimal variation. In one place there was a forgotten parasol, a pram, a rusty grill. Somewhere else well-trimmed evergreen trees grew. I had never seen it that way before, *the world*. Our little world, the blocks, the rows, the car park. Someone would tell them that Mussa was my friend. That he often stayed over at my place. They would come, I thought, lots of them in their dark uniforms. I changed my vantage point. On the other side of the building everything was as drab as the weather. Nothing to see. Through the kitchen window I looked up at the sky.

I sliced a bunch of bread and covered them with a jarful of jam. I filled a bottle of water before I woke him up. He lay for a moment collecting himself.

Where am I? he asked, and then everything came back to him. His hands began to shake.

Take off your clothes, I said.

I got him to change tops. Into one with a large hood to hide his face. I lent him a pair of jogging bottoms. We threw the old ones down the rubbish chute on our way out.

We have to hide until it gets dark, I said, and skipped the last step on the way down to the basement. I opened the door and fumbled for the switch. I don't need the light anyway, I managed to think before the fluorescent tubes in the ceiling flickered a couple of times. I grew up down there. In the corridors beneath the tower blocks, in the passages between numbers seven, nine and eleven, and then all the way round to the connecting passage. I started to run, and Mussa followed. Luckily the laundry room was empty. I hopped up on the tumble dryer and managed to coax open the hatch to the service tunnel. We crawled inside.

At the end of the tunnel we jumped out and found ourselves in a different block altogether. The cops don't know about this place, I whispered, and found Mussa's hand. They don't know shit, I said a little louder and opened a door that led to the network of paths, where we could move more or less unseen towards the school's abandoned athletics ground.

We can hide here, I told Mussa. I just know it.

Where? Mussa asked. We were standing on the football pitch in the twilight. The steep banks around the school's athletic stadium were like black whales enclosing the area.

Over there, behind the long jump, I said. The pipe. Can't you see the pipe?

Mussa nodded, but he couldn't see a thing. Not without his glasses.

What did you say? he asked.

Over there.

No, before that.

Just that I come here sometimes. That I come here to hide.

Mussa looked at me.

Just when things aren't going well at home, I continue.

Why are you doing this, Mussa asked. We crossed the football pitches, past the skate ramp, where the hawthorn stood like a naked witch in the winter darkness, then over to the long jump.

Because we have to get away.

I, Mussa said. I have to get away.

What does that mean?

That I'm going to Somalia.

Home?

Mussa pulled out a Rizla from the pack. We only had the short ones. He pulled out another one and skilfully licked the adhesive strip with just the right amount of saliva. I was familiar with his practised movements without being able to see him in the darkness. In a way I could sense it all with my body, feel it with the tip of my tongue and my fingers, him rolling everything tightly around a small piece of cardboard, an improvised roach.

There, Mussa said, and asked for the mix.

I held out my hand. He held the back of my hand and hesitated for a moment, then, with precise movements, filled the cone with the mix, dabbed at my palm and rubbed off the remaining crumbs in the dark.

Then came the flame, the smoke, the coughing.

...

I have no home, he said. It doesn't exist any more. Do you understand? It was razed when I was a baby. We fled across the desert. I don't know how we ended up here. Back then I was just a baby in a sling on my mother's back. I wasn't Mussa back then. I was just a pitiful creature at risk of dying in the heat, dying of thirst. Can you imagine that? Dying because there's no water? Or because your parents have to leave you lying in the sand. That was what my stepdad used to say when he hit me: They should have left you in the sand back then, he said, then I would have avoided all of this trouble.

Can you imagine that, Tim?

I could. He knew I could. I got up and felt the concrete against the top of my head.

Do you think they're coming? Mussa said.

Yeah, at some point, I answered. Have you got money?

A little, he answered. I've got my passport too.

Why did you do it?

There's always a limit, Mussa answered.

I sat down again. I found his hands in the dark.

Felt the blood.

It's like it's stuck to you, I said. Like we can't get it all off.

I started to scratch at my friend's hands. My nails scraped the surface of his pale palms.

I'm high.

I'm fucking high, Mussa said.

I'm cold, I replied.

Me too, Mussa said.

We heard the sirens. Mussa sat down by the mouth of the pipe and looked out into the autumn; the cold central pitch and the football goals were just visible in the distance. The wind had started up and a loose sheet on the skate ramp was beating out a strange rhythm.

It reminds me of summer, Mussa said. When we wanted to fasten the plate with a screw someone had brought from home. We didn't know what we were doing and we tried to screw it all the way down, but it didn't work properly so the head of the screw poked up.

I hurt my knee on that screw, he said.

That was the day we became friends.

We didn't know each other back then. We were in different classes.

Tim, Mussa said. Why did you talk to me?

I didn't answer. I sat down behind him. I put my arms round him.

Mussa was quiet.

He'd stood washing the blood off his shin. The wound from the screw had already formed a skin. He had taken off his Vans. They were flung across the asphalt.

Did you hurt yourself?, I asked.

What do you think? Mussa answered.

I knew what he was expecting.

Conflict. How he was seen from the outside and how he saw himself.

I knew it well. Being alone, feeling like you were surrounded by idiots.

I helped him switch off the water.

Do you want to come with me? I asked. Get away from here.

He looked at me and rolled down his trouser leg. The fabric was torn and soaked with blood.

You have to go to A & E, I said. You could get blood-poisoning, I continued, but he just stood staring at me stupidly.

I motioned. He did not react.

Then I said, Or can you deal with everything arse-up, talking to your friend *Allan*?

That was about all he could take.

What are you saying?

He walked towards me. Limping. I just stood there.

Why are you saying that shit? he asked.

Just for kicks. Come on. Let's cut class.

But Mussa did not find it funny. He turned and started to walk away.

Leave me alone, he said. Just piss off. That thing you said, you know.

He didn't finish his sentence.

I know, I said. Sorry, Mussa.

What did you say? Mussa stopped and turned around. You mean that, stupid Paki? he asked with a slight smile.

I nodded.

Mussa, I said, I mean every word I say.

And Christians never lie, right? he answered.

We gave each other a ghetto hug, just a light touch of the shoulders, two palms meeting and clasping.

And we left. Cycled into the centre. Into the town centre and behind the station where I showed him a place where a person could be left alone. It was a small enclosure where there used to be a rubbish container, back when the takeaway was still open.

They used to stand out here smoking, I said. I know. My mum used to work here. She would bring home broken sausages and chips. That was why we had those large containers of mustard and French dressing. And ketchup. That was why our flat always smelt like a deep-fat fryer.

We walked round a white building. A kind of pavilion. Behind the building was a small courtyard, covered by a kind of roof. Someone had placed a leather sofa against the wall and there was graffiti on the fence. There were cigarette butts everywhere. Empty cans.

Nobody will ever come here, I said. I mean, apart from me.

We sat down on the sofa.

We sat there.

We smoked and we became friends. It's easy enough when you have something in common like hardship. We talked about it. All the things we didn't have. Dads, for example.

My dad died at an asylum centre in Germany, Mussa said. He was run over. It started a small clan war, and my mum and I had to flee again. This time we moved in with a bastard who beat both of us. I was young. He forced me to call him Dad.

I went one better. Told him what it's like to be home. My home. What it's like to have a mum who drinks. One who's never home. Is depressed. All the times I couldn't be bothered to go home and my mum couldn't care less.

We sat on the leather sofa and became friends.

You pale shit, Mussa said with a laugh. You glow-in-the-dark pig lover.

Just then there was a flashing blue light by the car park at the back of the sports hall. We both saw it. The flashing was initially obscured by the hawthorn thicket, but then it formed clear, strong shafts of light that pierced the dusk.

They stopped, Mussa said.

They're coming now, we thought.

He grabbed my hand, but let go again, like he regretted it.

I pulled my friend back and kissed him. I pulled him into the darkness, we fell over.

It's a sin, Mussa said.

A lot of things are, I said. We're practising to be grown-ups. For the ladies.

Are you?

No. Are you?

Yes. I'm practising for the ladies.

When we sat up again, the blue flashing was gone and the world had calmed down.

Maybe I should go now, Mussa said.

They'll catch you, I answered. You won't even make it as far as the bus.

Translated from the Danish by Paul Russell Garrett

Illustrations by Serge Bloch

Breakwater

Michaela Holzinger

My father is like a migratory bird.

Each year he heads south in autumn, to the lake, where he spends his days playing chess under the cypress trees. My dad is a chess fanatic. Hardly anybody is a match for him, but there is one person: Walter Bleckman. He also holidays there at this time of year, and the two of them sit by the water for hours, immersed in their black-and-white world.

Although I'm not a migratory bird, and nor is my mum, we still have to go with him every time. Migratory birds don't like to fly alone. I'm sure that's why Walter Bleckman drags his wife and son along every time as well. Kilian's the same age as me. They all think that's splendid. I don't. I'm really fed up with their whole *Kilian & Lilian* shtick.

'Don't make that face,' Dad says as soon as we start loading the car. 'You've been playing with Kilian since you were just a little sprog.'

I don't reply to this, because it's been years and years since I was a little sprog: I'm fourteen now, which means it's mega-embarrassing hanging around with a spotty weirdo who could be my younger brother. Kilian seemed to get stuck in his Lego-Minecraft world years ago. When I think how just last year Dad even told me to *play* with Kilian a bit it makes me shudder. But time has a way of reshaping things, and not even my father can do anything about that, luckily.

When we arrive, our regular hotel is newly resplendent – an omen, maybe. Everything's fresh, everything's different. Dad grumbles; Mum and I are secretly delighted. To my father's chagrin, there's no family room; instead I get a single room with a view of the lake and a mould-free shower. The fruit basket beside the bed really puts me in a holiday mood. Perhaps it's not so bad here after all. Five days' lounging around on a king-size bed with a flat-screen TV does have a certain appeal, even if I'd rather have spent the autumn holiday with my best friend Zoe. At least my parents are leaving me alone. Dad's already sitting under the cypresses; Mum's meeting Bleckman's wife for coffee. No sign of Kilian.

Maybe this year the weirdo succeeded where I failed and has stayed at home, with the run of the house and a full fridge. Fuck! I roll out of bed, see the lake in all its glory and think: the lake can never be the sea. Not even the fruit basket can obscure that fact. Although… the lake used to be everything to us. Kilian and I used to play coastguard on the pier, which stretches so far out into the lake you sometimes actually get a few proper waves out there: the kind you get in the sea, waves that whisper of adventure. Our parents would never have allowed us to play on the slippery rocks. You really have to take care not to slip or graze your ankles. But we never slipped, and our ankles stayed in one piece, so the pier was our secret – for a while, anyway. Then it stopped being interesting, and so did Kilian.

I pull on my trainers. Looking out of the window, I've spotted a figure clambering about on the rocks of our pier. I turn my back on the king-size bed: I'd rather know who's still looking for adventure out there, among the waves.

This boy is bigger than the weirdo, I realize as I reach the shore. Added to which he's got muscles; in fact, this guy's really good-looking. I'm suddenly embarrassed that I crawled out of bed just as I was, with unbrushed hair and crumpled clothes. For a moment I consider turning back, but the lure of the pier has already taken hold, and I balance my way, surefooted, over the rocks. I dance out over the lake, farther and farther, and I've almost reached the end when the guy turns round. A surprised smile flits across his face, and I very nearly slip.

'Shit – Kilian, is that you?'

The guy with the tanned skin and two-metre-wide shoulders frowns. 'Who else would it be?' he asks in a deep voice. I flop down beside him on the last rock, where we used to sit shoulder to shoulder, imagining our sea had no end. It feels different now. The lake's not a sea, and Kilian's not a sprog. Kilian is suddenly... *hot*. The blood rushes to my face as I catch myself eyeing him up. Zoe would give him ten out of ten, and so would I. Kilian grins; the former weirdo seems to be enjoying the fact that he's not a weirdo any more.

Time is unpredictable sometimes: it takes great strides, and nobody notices.

'Autumn again,' he says casually. 'Your hair's got longer...'

Damn it, my hair's the same as always – I've been wearing it long for years. Kilian knows that perfectly well, and he also knows that he's hot all of a sudden. I narrow my eyes, and watch him grin even more broadly. That shakes me out of my astonishment. I punch his shoulder and burst out laughing.

'What have you been doing? Karate, and eating loads of spinach? You look' – I struggle to find a word that isn't *hot*, and blush again in the process – 'well... different. Taller.'

Kilian shrugs. 'So do you,' he answers tersely. Then we sit on our rock as if we're about to play coastguard again, but we don't. Instead, we have another idea. It drifts in of its own accord, but perhaps it's the current washing it up against the rocks. The pier breaks the waves; it's the way it interacts with the lake that's always fascinated us. Wordlessly we stick our feet in the foam-flecked water and sense the opportunity. Kilian & Lilian. We're on the same wavelength; we don't need to say much. The same thing every autumn for fourteen years – that's formative.

It's time to break the waves.

When migratory birds head south, they like to stop in places where they can find food. For our fathers, it's the Kumasi Restaurant. Every evening they drag us there, where they drink to the good old days and shamelessly chomp their way through the menu. Kilian and I politely play along: we're dressed up specially for them, after all. I've put on my ultra-short shorts and a skintight top; with his side cut and polo shirt Kilian looks about eighteen. We arrive together: time has played into our hands, we know our performance will be a success.

My dad promptly chokes on his aperitif. Kilian's father frowns as we join the table. So much for little sprogs. One-nil to us; the game has begun. Starters are served, our fathers recover from their initial shock, the atmosphere gets more relaxed – until Kilian puts his arm around me.

Dad clears his throat. 'Lilian, aren't you cold?' he asks, and notices, to his surprise, that over the past few years I must somehow have grown two breasts. His eyes are wide with consternation – well, the top I'm wearing is *so* tight, in ordinary circumstances I'd never wear it without a sweater. I almost feel sorry for my father.

'No,' I lie, held in Kilian's arm; it's warm, which disconcerts me.

Walter Bleckman sighs. 'How time flies. You two were still in nappies yesterday, weren't you?' He drinks to this, but it seems my father isn't thirsty any more. Helplessly he glances at my mother, who just smiles. She was there when I bought my first bra at the age

of twelve; she's known for ages that I'm not a little sprog any more, and nor is Kilian. He's the same age as me, after all.

Mr Kumasi himself serves the main course; we give our fathers a break, take our hands off each other and peel scampi. The rest of the evening passes amiably. Dad doesn't talk as much about chess, and nor does Walter Bleckman; instead, they listen when Kilian and I start chatting about music, and other stuff as well; my father's not the only one who's amazed.

For the first time ever, the next autumn morning doesn't begin with chess.

'What are you going to do today?' Dad asks at breakfast.

I pluck a croissant into bite-sized pieces and wash it down with orange juice. 'Dunno… maybe play with Kilian a bit?' I answer pertly.

Now Mum raises her head too. Suddenly I'm the lead migratory bird, the one that determines the direction of flight. There's nothing my parents can do but watch me fly away; there's no place for them where I'm going. I kiss them both on the cheek and flutter off towards my destination, the place of the whispering waves.

Kilian's already waiting. 'The plan's working,' he grins cheekily, seeming to grow taller before my very eyes as he does so. 'Mine talked about nothing else this morning except how tall you'd got.'

I look out over the water and marvel at how strange it is that change only becomes visible when it acquires a different face. I realize that I don't always recognize myself, either. How is it that time can fly and yet stand still? Kilian nudges me with his shoulder; a familiar feeling, yet somehow different. My questions are reflected in his eyes, but he grins them away. 'Come on – I'll show you something,' he says, and pulls me to my feet.

We clamber back to the beach and run up the narrow alleyways leading into the little town. From there we keep walking uphill until I'm completely out of breath. Kilian takes my hand, and I let him, although *Dad & Dad* are nowhere in sight. My hands are tingling, Kilian's hair is blowing in the wind; the remains of summer lie in the corners of the alleyways, time is playing tricks on me, everything's far away. Kilian stops in front of an enormous olive tree and looks up into its leaves. He helps me onto the branches and climbs up after me. From here, the lake is spread out at our feet; it's puckering into waves, the wind is whipping it up; our pier looks tiny from here.

'My favourite spot,' he murmurs, settling into the fork of two branches. I do the same, and we perch in the tree like migratory birds. How can we know what will be tomorrow when we don't understand today? I sigh.

Kilian searches my face for a smile. I ought to kiss him now, really, on the lips, because that's the game, but the moment is too special to complicate it with rules; we too are in the grip of the past. Kilian reaches for my hand, and we sit for a while watching the breakwater breaking waves, sighing into the wind together.

It's the last day of the autumn holiday. Tomorrow we'll be heading north, back home. Someone knocks on my bedroom door.

'Lilian, are you there?'

It's Dad. I'm surprised he's not sitting under the cypresses. 'Do you feel like coming to the old town with me? For a coffee, maybe?...' He smiles nervously. Mum must have put him up to it, but it's still nice that he's asked.

I nod and follow my father. He walks slowly: I'd never noticed that. At some point I take his arm and we adjust our speed; even though we don't talk much, it's OK like this. We eat cannoli in a little bistro; afterwards we go for a walk around town and stop in front of a shop window. 'Do you want to go in?' he asks.

'Sure, why not?' I answer, and browse around the little shop with him. He buys me a silver necklace with a pendant, and I'm happy that time has moments like this to spare as well.

When Dad puts the necklace around my neck he has to stand on tiptoe. 'You're not a little sprog any more,' he says, and from the way he says it it sounds as if he's OK with it, even though migratory birds don't like to fly alone.

But time is constantly moving forward, and soon the next day's upon us. We say goodbye to the Bleckmans: the migratory birds are flying again, obeying the rhythm, like the water in the lake.

The breakwater stays behind and breaks the waves.

Translated from the German by Charlotte Collins

Illustrations by Rotraut Susanne Berner

RMS *Titanic*

Nina E. Grøntvedt

'Can you imagine if I broke my *leg* too?!' Simon exclaims, before throwing himself dramatically from the stage and landing on his back on the crash mat down below. Several of the others laugh, because Simon looks so funny as he lies there, thrashing from side to side and playfully wailing 'ouch, ouch, ouuuch!' as he clutches one foot.

Simon is the clumsy, accident-prone class clown. Ever since we started primary school, he's broken one or another of his bones nine times! And that's in less than seven years! An arm, a leg, a finger, a toe, over and over again. It shouldn't be possible, but somehow it is. You see, Simon has the *worst* luck – in life, in love, in everything he does. He and Omar had tackled each other during last Wednesday's football match in PE. Omar ended up with a few bruises. Simon broke his arm. But a plaster cast won't stop Simon. He insisted on hanging on to his role for tomorrow's end-of-term performance, where he's due to act in a scene with Anna.

As Simon lies on the crash mat, howling and showing off, he's looking up at the stage. Up at her. Anna. She stands at the edge, glances down at Simon and smiles, but only just a little. Even so, he positively *beams* back up at her, moaning and groaning just that little bit more, desperate to hold her attention. Everyone can see that Simon is doing absolutely *everything* he can to get Anna to notice him. It's been that way for almost seven years now. Ever since the first day of their very first year at school, Anna has been the unattainable object of Simon's affections. *Everyone* can see it. Simon does nothing to hide it, either – he just can't. Unfortunately for Simon, everyone can also see that Anna doesn't feel the same way.

'That would be a full-blown disaster! Right, *Rose*?!' Simon proclaims at the top of his voice, gazing up at Anna with big Bambi eyes. 'Who'd be the Jack to your Rose if *that* were to happen, eh?! If I broke my leg, I mean?! A broken arm *and* a broken leg? Hmm? Rose? Anna?…'

Simon waves his plaster cast, which holds his arm at a permanent ninety-degree angle, just like a doll's arm. He waits for Anna to look back at him, to give him an answer. But Anna doesn't respond. She's busy talking to some of the others – Marcus and Leon, to be more precise. The boys have made their way up onto the stage, where they chat and joke and laugh and *flirt* with Anna. Well, they're doing their best to, in any case. It looks as if it might be working too, because Anna is giggling away. Simon looks hurt where he lies on the crash mat, but still he stares up at Anna, touching his leg and whimpering in the hope that she'll notice him again. But she doesn't notice him. Poor Simon, with his unrequited love for the most popular girl in class… No, the most popular girl in the whole *school*!

Simon isn't the only one in love with Anna, you see. *All* of the boys go weak at the knees for her, and probably some of the girls too. Anna is the kind of girl who can pick and choose between *whoever* she likes. And one thing is certain – she *doesn't* choose *Simon*.

'Shall we go through that one more time, then?' their teacher asks.

Simon is up on his feet in a flash, leaping onto the stage and standing at the ready. He lines himself up directly behind Anna, as close as he dares get without seeming creepy. Anna stands with her back to him, not looking at Simon and evidently not listening to their teacher either. She continues chatting away to Marcus and Leon. As she throws her head back in laughter at something Marcus says, Simon is whipped in the face by her long hair. But he doesn't move an inch. Instead he closes his eyes, and it looks as if he's *inhaling* the scent of Anna all the way up through his nostrils. Everyone can see him, of course – everyone but Anna.

'Anna?' the teacher says, coughing to get her attention.

Anna doesn't react in the slightest. She laughs and chats to Marcus and Leon as if they were the only three people in the world. Tough-guy Marcus, lovable Leon… and Anna. Maybe she's in love with one of them? They're certainly in love with her – that's as clear as day. Especially Leon, even if it's Marcus who talks the loudest and acts the toughest.

'Ahem, young Miss Anna Mork?' the teacher says sternly.

Anna leaps in the air and spins around, and as she does so her long hair flutters outwards and whips Simon in the face yet again, and he is in *heaven*. He gawps at Anna. Marcus and Leon gawp too. Actually, most people in the room do the same, and it's not all that unusual, because no matter what Anna does, it looks perfect. Just like something from a film. Only the teacher is wearing a strict and rather serious expression.

'Yes?' Anna replies, flashing the teacher her perfect movie-star smile.

'Can you let these young men get back to what they're supposed to be doing, so that you and Simon can go over this one more time, please?' the teacher asks.

'Of course!' Anna replies, beaming in the most *utterly* heartfelt way that makes even the teacher melt a little.

She turns to face Marcus and Leon, calling out 'Bye!' as she waves them off. The boys smile and Leon blushes as the two of them hop down from the stage and saunter off as casually as they can. Anna turns back to Simon, who starts grinning like an idiot. He just can't help himself, the poor thing.

Side by side, Anna and Simon make their way behind the stage curtain. Everything falls silent in the auditorium. Someone from the sound team switches on Celine Dion, and everyone looks up at the stage. Simon – or should I say *Jack* – enters first, wandering on stage all alone. He's tried combing his hair back in a side parting, just like Jack's in the film. He looks quite cute, really, though not a *handsome* kind of cute, more like a *cute-little-puppy-dog* kind of cute.

Jack looks as if he's deep in thought as he gazes out over the auditorium, which is supposed to be the sea. He doesn't notice Rose approaching him.

'Hello, Jack,' she says, and Jack jumps.

'Rose!' he exclaims, as he turns around hurriedly to face her.

'I changed my mind,' Rose says. 'They said you might be up here—'

'Shhh,' Jack says, interrupting her, but not in a rude way, more like with *passion*, before speaking again: 'Give me your hand.'

He reaches out an arm (the arm without the plaster cast) and offers his hand to Rose, who looks at it cautiously. She locks eyes with Jack and asks:

'What are we going to do?'

'Step up and hold on to this railing,' Jack replies, dashingly.

He points at a spot in thin air, since there's no actual railing on stage. Rose sees the invisible railing all the same, and takes a step in Jack's direction. His face breaks into a wide smile, his arm still outstretched. The entire auditorium waits with bated breath. Then, *finally*, Rose takes Jack's hand, and he carefully leads her out towards the edge of the stage, where they unsteadily pretend to clamber up onto a railing that isn't actually there.

'Oh, look at the ocean!' Rose exclaims, and they gaze out at the entire seventh grade, every single one of them watching.

'Close your eyes,' Jack says.

'But why…' Rose begins.

'Just close your eyes,' Jack tells her.

Rose closes her eyes and smiles nervously. Jack stands behind her, so close that his lips are just by her ear, then says:

'Hey, don't peek! Do you trust me?'

Jack places two trembling hands on Rose's waist. She laughs as if it tickles, and Jack actually blushes! As red as a *tomato*!

'I trust you,' Rose replies tenderly, and leans her head back slightly to one side, in his direction.

Jack takes her arms, extending them out on either side of her. She flinches slightly with surprise, but keeps her eyes closed. The two of them stand there, their fingers interlaced, each of them with their arms outstretched and it's… so… romantic. Or rather… they stand there, their fingers interlaced, their arms outstretched *on one side*, while on the other side only Rose's arm is fully extended and Jack's arm in its plaster cast is well and truly stuck at a ninety-degree angle, holding Rose slightly unnaturally somewhere by her elbow.

'OK, open your eyes,' Jack says, his voice trembling.

Jack *glows* with love for Rose, whom he holds by the hand and elbow respectively. Rose opens her eyes slowly. She gazes outward with her arms outstretched and suddenly exclaims with delight:

'Oh! I'm flying, Jack! I'm flyyyyyying!'

And as she says the words, the two of them lose their balance, tumble over the edge with a howl and disappear...

... to the *alarm* of everyone in the auditorium, because they just fell in the *sea*! Before they could even kiss or *anything*! Everyone claps, the whole room whistling and cheering. Simon and Anna lie on the crash mat giggling as Simon gazes at her longingly. He's so *completely* captivated by her...

'Anna!' Clara calls out, as she and a couple of others from the costume group make their way into the auditorium carrying some bags.

Clara holds up a long navy dress. Anna stands up and runs over to see them, while Simon remains where he is on the crash mat.

'Wooow!' Anna exclaims. 'It's soooo nice!'

She holds the dress up in front of her and gives a twirl, and both the dress and her hair flutter all around her. It's the dress she'll be wearing when she plays Rose. The end-of-term performance has become quite the professional affair. The costume team have kept themselves busy, borrowing all sorts of things from parents of everyone in the year group. They've sent out emails with lists of everything they need and have already collected a mountain of clothing and other bits and pieces. There are some really cool things. Rose's dress, for instance – it's *so* 1912.

'Hey, do you have my costume there?' Simon calls out to them, jogging over to Anna and the others.

'Nope, sorry!' Clara tells him.

'Ah, that's a shame...' Simon replies.

Everyone knows that he doesn't really care about his costume. He only ran over because Anna is standing there. Even so, she doesn't look at him. She's completely absorbed by the long blue dress.

'You guys!' Marcus shouts, whistling to get everybody's attention. 'Can everyone sit down? We've got a surprise for you all!'

Marcus and Leon are standing on stage, looking out at their audience with a mysterious air. People glance quizzically around the room and take their seats. Leon brings down the big screen as Marcus explains that they've been working as part of an undercover film crew! In complete and total secret, they've been shooting a behind-the-scenes film, a film they're now going to play for everyone! A pre-premiere before the film's actual premiere at the end-of-term show tomorrow, just so they can make sure everything goes to plan and that kind of thing. Anticipation is high as everyone looks up at the screen and the film begins.

After a while, it becomes clear that Simon and Anna have been filmed a lot more than the others in the year group. Clip after clip shows just the two of them, with Simon gazing wistfully at Anna as Anna looks elsewhere. Simon following Anna around. Simon standing beside Anna. Simon talking to Anna, showing off around her, laughing at *everything* she says, regardless of whether it's funny or not, and during the entire time she fails to notice him at all. All of a sudden, the atmosphere in the auditorium feels uneasy. Anna sits whispering with some of her friends. Simon stares straight ahead. He doesn't look as if he knows what to say or do, and then, before he manages to say or do anything at all, a new film clip begins, showing Simon on his own this time, clearly with no idea that he's being filmed. He stands there dancing wildly, his arms and legs flailing as he rocks out with his headphones on, and singing too, screeching off-key as he listens to the music. Several people in the auditorium laugh, because Simon just looks so funny. He's not the class clown for nothing. All of a sudden, the Simon on screen realizes he's being filmed, leaps in the air and looks a *teeny* bit self-conscious before smirking at the camera and pushing a hand towards it, the screen turning black before the camera is switched off...

Everyone bursts out laughing – including Simon – because it was just so hilarious. As the bell rings to signal that it's break time, the credits roll and various pictures of the film crew show up on screen, all of them grinning, waving and giving the audience the thumbs-up to delighted cheers and applause. Anna sits with a big group all around her. They whisper and giggle together. They stare at Simon all the while, who pretends not to notice, though of course he does. And for the first time in almost seven years, Simon appears to be embarrassed. He had seen the film – *everyone* had seen it (!) – and now they *all* know just how pathetic he really is. Simon gets up and makes his way towards the door. Because why should he stay? Anna doesn't notice him. She never will. Not in the way that he notices her. Just before he reaches the door, he stops and turns around. He looks at something. Or, not *something*, but *someone*. Of course. Simon can't leave the room without one last look at Anna. It's impossible for him not to, even after having made a fool of himself on screen like that.

And Anna? She's busy with her friends, at least until Marcus approaches her. Then all of a sudden she's busy with Marcus, who is cool and confident, and *funny*, as usual, and all without even trying. Without having to be a clown. Marcus says something and Anna bursts into a fit of giggles. Simon is still standing on the other side of the room watching them, and he looks crushed, as if he finally, *finally*, after seven long years, has realized that he hasn't a single chance with her, that he and Anna will *never* be together… not ever. Marcus says a few more things that Anna laughs at, all without a single glance in Simon's direction. When Simon finally turns around, he hangs his head and makes his way towards the door all alone…

There's only one day left of primary school, and nobody can say that Simon hasn't tried. But when it came to Anna, he didn't ever quite succeed. It's almost enough to make someone want to cry. Like watching a film. A really, really *sad* film… Like, *look out, there goes the loser!* Simon, who never managed to win the heart of the target of his affections, the sad kid standing all alone, with a broken arm, even – what a cliché!

'SIMON!' someone shouts all of a sudden.

Simon spins around. It was *Anna*! And now she's running in his direction, straight towards him, calling out to him.

'I need to write something on your plaster cast!'

And Simon lights up! He stands up tall once again! Anna stops in front of him. She's got a marker pen in one hand and writes him a message. Simon is on the brink of *exploding* with happiness. Anna finishes up writing and gives Simon a hug (!) before turning round and running off again. Simon seems totally…. totally… well, *speechless*. Anna even does a little pirouette, as she smiles and waves to him, before rejoining her friends. Simon simply stands there gaping, and he can't help himself from grinning. Eventually he snaps out of it and looks down at his plaster cast. He reads the words over and over and over again. 'Your Rose,' it says, followed by a winking smiley face and a heart, all in blue marker pen.

As Simon skips through the doorway, light on his feet, Anna calls out to him:

'And don't you go breaking your foot before tomorrow, Jack!'

Translated from the Norwegian by Rosie Hedger

Illustrations by Ella Okstad

Everyone Knows Petter's Gay

Endre Lund Eriksen

Petter had stuck to me like glue ever since he moved here last autumn. I think I was the first to make eye contact with him in the schoolyard. Just to be nice, I gave him a smile and a nod.

I'd have to pay for that gesture every single day. Whenever he caught sight of me, he flashed a smile and winked, as if we were *such* good friends. He was so bubbling over with joy whenever he saw me that I felt like a million-dollar celebrity. The problem was, though, that when he spoke he sounded so loud and shrill that he attracted a lot of attention I'd rather do without. Whenever I stood chatting to him, I got the feeling the whole playground could hear what he was saying in that high-pitched, pathetic voice of his, and they could all see I was the one talking to him.

Fortunately he wasn't in my class, so I saw him mostly at break times and in the park where we played in the evenings. He turned up with a big grin and wide, shining eyes, and asked very nicely if he could hang out with us. After a while, some idiot or other asked him if he wanted to join our football team. He came to every single training session, never even skipped one, and was always there fifteen minutes or half an hour early to do some extra practice on his own. Talk about sucking up to the coach!

Every time he saw me, whether at training or in the schoolyard, he clung to me like a limpet. In the changing room he always managed to squeeze into the space beside me, or turn up in the showers right beside where I was standing, always blabbering on in that over-enthusiastic, cheerful voice of his. He was nice enough, in a grov-elling, pestering kind of way, and no matter what I said, his answer was always, 'brilliant!', 'cool!', or 'that's just fantastic!' At first it was kind of infectious, and I was incredibly excited about talking to him. But that passed quickly, especially after the coach got it into his head to put Petter in midfield instead of me. It was actually only to be friendly – after all the coach tries to include everyone, or at least give everyone a chance – but eventually he showed off so much in midfield that he thought he lived there. He had some luck with a few counter-attacks and scored a couple of goals, and all of a sudden I was shifted to the back, even though I'd trained loads to get fit so that I could run backwards and forwards for two stints of forty-five minutes, and perfected my long passes up to Helge from midfield.

It wasn't that I was jealous or anything. If he'd been better than me, it would've been OK – like Helge, who's born to be a striker, fast and accurate, though he's not in especially great shape. But Petter was clumsy and inaccurate; half the time he missed when he passed the ball to Helge, and he always apologized in that over-the-top, happy voice of his: 'Sorry, mate!' Or: 'My fault! Won't happen again!' Heaven only knows why the coach let him pitch camp in my spot, because passing to Petter was a game of chance that ended seventy per cent of times with him tripping over the ball or kicking it out over the sideline.

He kept dropping hints about me coming over to his place and tried to wangle his way into visiting me, with ill-concealed questions about where I lived and whether I had any brothers or sisters, that kind of thing. But I made out I didn't understand, and eventually he stopped hassling me.

Instead he began to hang out with Therese Dahl and her lot. He stood with them at break times, tagged along with them on the way to and from school, and it was Therese Dahl and her crowd he arrived with at the Club on Fridays. He danced with them too, and not just slowly, like you have to if you're going to do a bit of snogging. Completely of his own accord, he'd stand out on the dance floor, stamping his feet to the rhythm while swinging his arms and legs and rolling his hips to make his enormous belt buckle sparkle. Always with that soppy grin on his face and a thousand stars twinkling in his eyes, making him look as sweet as a baby doll.

He got the beat and all that, and he knew some moves that looked pretty cool. I mean, if you like that sort of thing. And it wasn't that I stood there staring or anything, but when you're hanging about waiting your turn to play snooker or air hockey, you can't help taking in a few things. Honestly, it was fucking annoying that someone so sissy and soft had girls swarming around him all the time.

'No idea what they see in him,' I said to Helge one night at the Club, as we lined up along the wall to watch the girls dancing, something that was pretty well ruined by *him* grinding his hips at them.

'Don't you get it?' Helge answered, taken aback. 'He's one of them, don't you see?'

'What do you mean?'

The way Helge looked at me, waggling his eyebrows like hula dancers from Hawaii or something like that, forced me to understand exactly what he meant: Petter was gay.

Helge was surprised I hadn't twigged, but actually I'd known all along: I just hadn't put two and two together yet. It was completely logical, because there was something girly about him, his features were soft and pretty, and the noise he made when he laughed wasn't real laughter but giggles. Everyone knew what he was; maybe I was just a bit slower on the uptake, so I'd stood talking to him at one break after another, while people probably drew their own conclusions.

That was why I hadn't liked those looks he sent me, I realized that now. The gay guy was out to get me.

* * *

When I found out that the coach had picked Petter for the district training camp, I was so pissed off that I almost couldn't care less that I'd been selected as well. There must be some sort of quota thing, a rule that they had to include, like, a Sami, a gay boy and an immigrant. It's not that he was useless – on a good day he was OK – but he wasn't bloody good enough for the *district team*. I *wasn't* scared of the competition, I *knew* that I was far better, but I knew that training camp was going to be a golden opportunity for him.

We were to spend the night at a school, and I made sure to put my roll mat, sleeping bag and sports bag far away from his belongings. It was an all-boys get-together, so he was probably lonely without the gang of girls he always had around him. Helge was the only other player from our team, but there were a few boys we knew from school, and we stayed together and made up our minds to support one another and stick together no matter who was chosen in the end for the district team. And while the rest of us high-fived and slapped one other on the back, Petter appeared out of nowhere and came over to high-five us and be one of the boys. When he tried to smack his fist against mine, I turned and walked away.

It was really fucking hard to focus on the game when I knew that the gay kid was staring at me no matter what I did. I noticed it as soon as we started warming up. Every time I threw a glance in his direction, he tried to make eye contact and land a smile on me. I refused to give him that pleasure. And as soon as the game was in full flow – and of course I had ended up in his team – as a matter of principle I avoided passing to him. Of course, he couldn't possibly think a pass from me was symbolic in any way – some kind of foot-flirting, so to speak – but, rather than ever send the ball his way, I gave other players these impossible passes, or else just fired off in the general direction of the goal.

Of course my playing was rubbish and I got parked on the bench, where I did my best to ignore Petter, even though of course it was his lucky day and he ran like a crazy golden retriever after the ball no matter where it rolled. While I stared at my phone to avoid seeing his shining eyes, he naturally managed to poke the ball into the net. It was obvious the way things were going. He was going to be picked, and I would be sent home with a derisory 'thanks for your efforts'.

So I decided to unmask him.

'Hey, isn't it weird they let that gay kid shower in the same changing room as us?' I said to the boys sitting beside me with their eyes fixed conscientiously on the football pitch.

No one answered. There was nobody from my school here on the bench, and the others who knew what kind of boy Petter was were running around on the field with him.

'Petter over there,' I explained. 'The one who's got possession now, everybody knows he's gay, so don't you think it's a bit weird for him to take a shower with us?'

As things turned out, the boy sitting next to me, a Somali so skinny that he looked like a daddy-long-legs, went to the school that Petter had attended before.

'No, Petter had a girlfriend last year,' he claimed. 'Kathinka, she was called. Fucking gorgeous, in fact.'

'You're kidding!' I said. 'Nah, that guy's definitely gay – you can smell it a mile off!'

'So what?' muttered some halfwit on the sidelines who was playing keepy-uppy with a ball beyond the bench.

Daddy-long-legs said that Petter and that girl called Kathinka had been together for a few months, and that they'd stood necking in more or less all the breaks at school, so he really doubted that Petter was gay. I thought I was going to blow a fuse.

'Then he's taken a tumble out of the closet since that time, because at our school everyone knows Petter's gay – just ask Helge.'

But Helge was out on the football field and impossible to contact.

'You can just see it in him,' I said.

The keepy-uppy guy stopped playing with the ball, and the others all stared out at the pitch. By chance Petter had got lucky with a sprint and was about to score.

'I don't think he looks gay,' said the keepy-uppy guy.

'But he plays well,' the Somali said.

So I was forced to prove it. People really need to know who they're going to take a shower with while they're stark-bollock naked.

* * *

I had to do it in the showers, right after the training session. I'd told the others and we'd rehearsed the signal – I was going to whistle when they were to come in to see how right I was. Until then, they were to look anywhere other than at Petter.

'You wouldn't dare!' Helge said as we headed into the changing room and he found out what was going on.

'D'you want to bet?' I asked him.

I could see in his eyes that he was impressed. And he laughed off the wager, because he realized he would lose. When I've really made up my mind to do something, I just go ahead and do it.

'What if you actually like it?' he teased me.

'Yeah, right!' I said.

* * *

Petter lagged behind as we went into the changing room, so I had to take my time getting undressed. All the others were in the showers and some of them were on their way out with towels round their waists when he finally arrived. He was with the coach, in the midst of a discussion about strategy or technique; of course he was jabbering away in that sparkling, happy voice of his, so positive and cheerful, so chock-full of team spirit and morale that it positively oozed out of his mouth in a stream of words.

I peeled off my clothes, slowly. Although the coach had unlocked the teacher's changing room and was well on his way through the door, Petter did not take the hint. He went on blabbering, and the coach (who, to be fair, had sat on the subs' bench for top-flight Tromsø IL the last time they were in the Cup Final) was politely struggling to round off the conversation. I took my towel and dived into the showers, exchanging glances with the Somali, who rushed to finish so that there would be two free places side by side, as we had arranged.

But Petter was dawdling outside. He took plenty of time, as if he'd suddenly turned shy. Even though the coach had obviously gone into his changing room and their conversation had finished ages ago, it took an eternity for Petter finally to step inside the shower room, towel round his waist. The others had left the showers long before, so Petter and I were alone. He hung his towel on one of the pegs and walked past me, turning away slightly, into the shower two down from the one where I was standing. I needed an excuse to get closer to him, so I commented that he'd played well today, and made sure to speak softly, so that he would have to say 'Eh?' With that, I had a cast-iron reason to move to the shower next to his. I turned it on and, as soon as the water was warm enough, I launched into a long speech praising his efforts and the goal he'd scored and all about the absolutely superb stuff he had done on the football pitch.

At first he didn't say anything, just rubbed shampoo into his hair and his armpits and down towards his crotch, letting the shower spray rinse it all clean. Eventually I lost my spark and ran out of words – it wasn't *that* easy to find great things to say about him.

But then he turned to face me.

'You know, I really thought you didn't like me.'

He said it in a broken voice, sort of sad. And that was unexpected, coming from someone who was always hyper with happiness.

'No, no!' I said. 'I *do* like you,' I told him, but he didn't seem convinced. When he looked at me, a furrow appeared between his eyes, a crack of sadness sort of thing. I almost felt a bit sorry for him, and had to force out a smile. But I was afraid it looked lopsided and false, so I concentrated hard on making it natural and friendly and kind of… what – flirty?

I stared at his lips, full and soft and outlined by tiny, jagged bristles. I knew I had to imagine they belonged to some beautiful woman if I was to succeed with this. But it was so going to be worth it. Soon everybody would know what kind of guy he was, and he was going to go through total hell if he did get selected for this fucking district team. I just had to kiss him and show the others that he liked it…

'I *really* like you,' I said, focusing my mind on this absolutely gorgeous girl I knew.

'I can see that,' he said, with a downward nod of his head.

To my crotch, where an old friend was sticking up in the air in a perversely resolute fashion.

I felt a blush spread over my cheeks, stinging like flames.

Petter left the showers.

I stammered something. I don't quite remember what. 'It's not what you think' or something. But when I wheeled round towards him, the whole fucking team was huddled in the doorway, gawking, even though I hadn't whistled the signal.

I spun away from them, but it was too late.

God, how they smirked.

I tried to laugh along with them, shouting after them about what a good trick I had played. But they only laughed even harder. 'What an arse!' one of them said. 'You're off your bloody head,' said another.

And then they disappeared from the doorway, and the only one left standing there was Helge, who did not laugh, who did not say anything, but just glared fiercely at me before tearing himself away and leaving without a word.

* * *

After that, we never spoke of it again, Helge and I. But all the others talked about it, they all laughed behind my back when I walked by at break times.

And of course, Petter was picked for that fucking district team, and soon afterwards he set out to get himself a girlfriend, making sure to snog her in the middle of the playground at every single school break. It was all nothing more than pretence, so that no one would realize. I tried to get a girlfriend too, but it's not bloody easy to get a girl when everyone's going around thinking you're gay.

Translated from the Norwegian by Anne Bruce

Illustrations by Jörg Mühle

Heads or Tails

Elisabeth Steinkellner

1

'Heads or tails,' said Paul. 'Heads we go, tails we stay here.'

I looked at him. A grain of sand was stuck in the corner of his eye, and I felt the urge to wipe it away carefully with the tip of my finger and rub it between my fingers. The way mothers might do with their children.

'I'm not sure,' I replied. I reached for his hand instead of his eye, and our fingers automatically interlocked.

A question flared for a moment in my mind: where does tenderness end and habit begin? But it was just a tentative flicker, nothing more.

Outside the window the cherry tree was blossoming with such shameless delight it almost made me angry.

'Spring is overrated,' I grumbled. 'All this sprouting and blossoming, it just makes people crazy.'

Paul looked at me in surprise.

'I think spring's a good time for a trip,' he said finally. 'Not too hot and not too cold.'

'Maybe,' I retorted.

'Come on, then,' he urged. 'We'll toss a coin.'

'OK, fine,' I said, thinking: five days. Just the two of us. All day and all night.

And the idea made me feel nothing at all.

Paul tossed the coin high in the air, startling a fly; it buzzed madly around the room, a big fat bluebottle. Paul caught the coin again and smacked it on the back of the other hand.

I didn't look; instead I watched the fly, which had just settled on the window pane, and silently gave it another three days.

2

I circled the bus-stop sign with my eyes: once, twice, again and again. The smell of lilac filled my nostrils and the twittering of birds was in my ears.

Quickly I put in my earphones.

'Music?' I asked, and Paul nodded, so I pulled one of the earplugs out again and held it out to him.

Then I scrolled through the albums on my phone, couldn't decide and eventually pressed *shuffle*.

This same song had come on the radio a few months ago, as Paul and I were perched on the edge of the sink waiting for the bread to pop up out of the toaster. Like a summer hit that had lost its bearings and wandered into winter. We'd drummed our heels in time with the music on the kitchen cupboard beneath, gazing out of the window at the thickly falling snow. And then we'd made plans for where we wanted to go in the summer. Five weeks, just the two of us, all day and all night, we'd said, and inside I was shouting for joy.

I glanced over at Paul. I would have liked to have known what he was thinking, whether he was remembering it too.

But he was looking down at the ground.

What if I were to meet him here and now, for the first time... I wondered.

And I knew: I'd still notice him immediately. He'd still be exactly my type.

I wanted to reach for his hand, but my arm wouldn't move, not towards him, so our arms went on dangling half a metre apart.

But the longer I looked at his hand, the more convinced I was that I would be one-hundred-per-cent certain to recognize it as his, among maybe even a thousand others.

The bus arrived, Paul glanced up, and when we smiled at each other there was a strange sense of embarrassment.

3

'We'll be seventeen soon,' said Paul, more to his own reflection in the window than to me. 'At last.'

'What do you think is going to be so very different at seventeen?' I replied.

He shrugged. 'Everything,' he said. 'The whole of life.' And grinned at me.

I leant my head on his shoulder. 'Everything,' I whispered, to see how it felt.

Everything. Everything. Everything.

'I like the whorl in your hair,' Paul declared, placing his finger on the spot on my head. This whorl that had never made a particular impression on anyone apart from him.

'I noticed it straight away,' he said. As if he'd read my thoughts.

'I know,' I said.

'I liked it right from the beginning,' he said.

'I liked *you* right from the beginning,' I said, closed my eyes, and let the movement of the bus rock me into tiredness.

At one point, Paul murmured, 'Maybe I'll drop out of school,' and I wasn't sure whether he'd said it for real or just in my dream.

'You don't mean that,' I replied.

He said nothing, and I didn't press him.

I just thought: it's Paul's idea of the week. He'll have a new one in a few days. As per usual. I looked out of the window: outside, the landscape was slipping past, and everything blurred before my eyes.

'I'm dizzy,' I said. More to my own reflection in the window than to him.

4

When we got off the bus it was already dark.

I felt dazed and my legs were stiff, and apparently it was the same for Paul, because both of us were stumbling down the street and kept bumping into one another. It was only when we put our arms round each other that we settled into a calmer rhythm.

We walked. And walked, for as long as our silence lasted.

It lasted too long, because eventually we reached the edge of town. There was nothing here, just blackness instead of houses.

'Why are we here?' I asked. 'I mean, generally. What are we doing here, in the middle of nowhere?'

Paul looked at me in surprise. 'Nothing,' he answered. 'Absolutely nothing. Just being together.'

'I'm hungry,' I muttered. I turned round and strode on ahead, back into the town that was scarcely deserving of the name.

He followed me. I tried to stay one step ahead of him, but eventually he just grabbed my jacket and held me back.

And I was glad he did.

Back at the main square we looked around. The supermarket seemed to be closing, but Paul ran over and quickly slipped in through the doors.

I went over to the fountain in the middle of the square and sat down on the stone steps. Instantly I felt the cold permeate my jeans.

Cystitis, I thought, or worse. And stayed sitting.

Paul came over, sat down beside me and spread his purchases out between us. He'd got everything I usually liked best of all.

Just not right now.

5

'Have *you*?' he wanted to know.

'I asked first,' I said, not letting it drop.

Paul frowned. 'What on earth gave you that idea?'

'Just wondering,' I answered. 'Well?'

He looked at me thoughtfully.

'Do we have to talk about it *now*?' he said at last. He turned away from me, and the bedsprings squeaked as if trying to shift our minds to other things.

'No, we don't have to,' I said. I tried to make it sound indifferent. As if it were just a question of whether he'd ever peed in a swimming pool.

A strip of skin peeped out between his t-shirt and jeans, and a few fine hairs glowed in the weak light of the bedside lamp.

I got up from the bed, went into the bathroom, undressed and stood under the shower. The water splashed down on my head and I tried to think of nothing.

I stood like that for an eternity, and when finally I pulled back the shower curtain Paul was sitting on the closed lid of the toilet, looking at me.

I paused in mid-gesture and stood there, motionless, wishing he were wearing a different expression. A less honest one. One that would deceive me and keep the truth from me.

Because what was I supposed to do with his answer?

And did it have to be now, with me naked and freezing? Unprotected from his 'yes'? How stupid of me even to have asked.

Paul rubbed his temples and stared at the ground. I felt my heart pounding in my ears.

At last he looked up, looked straight at me and said: 'No.'

6

The next morning we awoke closely entwined.

I peeled myself out of Paul's arms and went to the toilet. My skin smelt of his sweat, and for a moment it occurred to me that perhaps everything might be all right, if only someone would stop time and we could live happy and contented for ever in our five-day bubble.

We left the bed-and-breakfast, and very soon we were both so hot that we stuffed our jackets and pullovers into our rucksacks.

Paul seemed to know where he wanted to go. I was happy not to have to deal with anything; I just walked beside him and didn't ask any questions.

We got on the bus, held up our tickets and stretched out, triumphant, along the entire length of the back seat.

We dozed. Ate the rest of our provisions. Wrote words on each other's palms with the tips of our fingers. Clicked through YouTube videos. Kissed. More intensely than the elderly couple in the row in front would have liked.

Eventually we got off again and boarded a train.

'Where are we actually going?' I asked Paul, but he just smiled mysteriously and squeezed my hand.

I leant back in my seat.

The rain came as if out of nowhere; it ran down the window panes in countless trails. Sometimes two drops united and flowed on together for a little while before their paths separated again.

It was only when the station signs changed colour that I realized we were already over the border.

Wordlessly, I looked at Paul. I didn't have to tell him that our tickets were no longer valid here.

He turned to face me, and smiled – a smile that was somewhere between excited and guilty.

And I understood: this was *his* journey.

Not ours any more.

7

We got off the train, and I had difficulty keeping up with Paul. He snaked through the crowds in the train station so purposefully that I suddenly felt out of place at his side.

As we stepped outdoors it almost felt like summer.

Paul was bounding along, whereas my rucksack weighed heavier and heavier on my shoulders. My rucksack, and the weight of all the unspoken questions.

Paul, where is it you actually want to go?

I mean generally, in life?

And am *I* there too, in your dreams for the future?

And is your answer from yesterday true – have you really not slept with anyone else since the two of us have been together?

Although… does that even matter any more?

'Paul,' I said, stopping abruptly, so that someone behind me stepped on my heels and swore, in a foreign language. 'We really need to talk.'

Paul turned to me and asked, 'Talk about what?'

'Well,' I began, 'I mean… Where exactly is it you're going?'

He raised his eyebrows, uncomprehending. 'Just towards the centre of town, to find a hostel or something.'

I nodded and looked at the ground, because I didn't know where else to look.

'Hey,' he said gently. He came over to me and put his arms around my waist. 'Would you rather have gone somewhere else?'

'No,' I answered, 'it's not that. It's great here—'

'Yeah,' he interrupted, 'it is, isn't it?'

I looked at him, sensing his enthusiasm, how relaxed he was. I wanted it to be infectious.

Maybe it really was that simple.

8

Paul pressed a poison-green drink into my hand, and I remembered reading somewhere that in the beginning the all-or-nothing principle applies, so I downed it in one.

Music boomed out on all sides. Paul dragged me onto the dance floor, closed his eyes and went with the crowd; and I copied him, sensing the alcohol and the heat in me, letting myself be caught up in the rhythm. Thoughts flowed away, and all that was left was the beat in my head and the vibration of the floor beneath my feet.

Until suddenly an elbow rammed into my side.

Not terribly hard, not so it really hurt, but still I felt the sudden urge to wrap my arms protectively around my body.

It was a few seconds before I realized what that meant.

Then I pushed my way through the crowd, ran outside, stuck my finger down my throat and vomited onto the pavement.

Paul followed me and stroked my back.

'Let's go,' I pleaded, and we walked hand in hand through the town, losing ourselves in the maze of narrow alleys.

'We could sign up to work on a ship,' said Paul, 'and sail around the world.'

I didn't need to look at him to know he wasn't joking.

'What I said about school,' he began, and I finished the sentence in my head. He'd meant it.

'You're sixteen,' I reminded him.

'Seventeen, in a few weeks,' he replied, 'and I don't want to sit around poring over a pile of books any more. I want to see *real* life at last.' He stopped and looked at me cautiously. 'Can you understand that?'

And what'll become of us? I wanted to ask, but all I could manage was a sob.

Real life, I thought. You can have that if you want, but quite differently to the way you imagine.

'We could – the two of us, together...' he said, drawing me into his arms.

9

I woke at dawn, freezing.

The room smelt of alcohol and the sweat of at least five other people, and I immediately felt sick.

I clambered down from the top bunk to join Paul and clung to him, so close I could feel his heartbeat. I lay there like that until it was light and the noise of traffic outside got louder.

Then I made a decision, and woke Paul.

'But why do you want to go back already?' he asked, for the umpteenth time, as we walked through town towards the station. 'School doesn't start for another two days.'

We entered the station building. I bought a ticket, and he trotted along behind me to the platform.

'Paul,' I said, surprised by the calmness in my voice, 'I'm not going to travel round the world. I've made my decision.'

He stood there, arms dangling, looking at the ground.

'And you have to make yours,' I whispered. I twisted a coin between my fingers in my trouser pocket, and thought: heads or tails.

Heads he stays; tails he comes with me. And then I'll tell him what I've wanted to tell him for days, and perhaps he'll be taken aback to start with, but then he'll be happy and say: well, if this isn't real life!…

He looked up, looked past me, into space, and said: 'I can't decide right now.'

I had to struggle to swallow the rising tears and stop my legs buckling beneath me.

When the train pulled in we hugged each other, and for a moment I wished Paul would just hold on to me and not let me board.

But he let me go, and I boarded, and the doors closed behind me.

Paul pressed his lips against the outside of the glass, and I pressed mine against the inside, and we kissed like that for several minutes, maybe; but it was only as the train began to move that it occurred to me that kiss might have been our last.

Translated from the German by Charlotte Collins

Illustrations by Hanne Kvist

Distance

Salla Simukka

'Sometimes the greatest journey is the distance between two people.'
  'The worst distance between two people is misunderstanding.'
  'The journey is more important than the destination.'
  For some reason these three phrases had pounded in my head all summer. They repeated like clockwork every day as I biked the fifteen kilometres from Turku to Naantali and back. I didn't know why they were such a persistent earworm. Maybe it had something to do with being twenty-one years old. Two years ago I had moved out of the house to another city to go to school, and by every objective yardstick I should have felt like an independent adult now, but most of the time I just felt lost. I was groping my way through life; I felt adrift and incomplete in every possible way.
  On a journey.
  Distant.
  Close.
  Not quite arrived.

I straightened the collar of my Mymble costume. I'd probably done that ten times already today, and I'd only been at work for two hours. The adjustment was an automatic hand motion these days. I didn't even notice it enough to be irritated any more. All of us working here fixed each other's collars on the fly too. If someone was working the till, someone else walking behind her might gently tug her collar back into position. It was a sign of solidarity. Everyone hated the detachable horrors.

I couldn't say I would have liked the costume even without the collar issue. The particular shade of pink and the tent shape didn't flatter anyone. The big buttons came undone easily and the edges of the pockets frayed. The thin but non-breathable synthetic fabric was cold on chilly days and hot on warm ones. But I could have endured all of this, even the collar constantly slipping out of place, if we had actually been playing Mymble, if we had actually been in character. We weren't. We were working at Moominworld, but we were merely sales staff in the gift shop. All we did was unpack boxes of incoming merchandise, stock displays and run the till. We were customer-service workers, not actors.

Of course it was a relief not to have to play a whimsical romantic like Mymble. I don't know if I would have even known how. I certainly wouldn't have been able to stay in character day after day. I had gone to a performing-arts high school, but I had never wanted to become an actor.

I already had to pretend to be enough things in my life. Older, stronger, wiser, funnier.

I complained about the outfits at the end of last summer, and I would complain at the end of this summer too when it was time to give feedback. I argued for getting rid of them based on their impracticality and that it was illogical for the children, because we were wearing costumes but weren't in character, which broke the illusion the amusement park was trying to create. It was also unfair that the only boy who worked in the shop, Lauri, got to wear a Moominworld T-shirt as his uniform. That would have been a perfect uniform for all of us.

I went to the stock room and started to unpack the boxes of toy balls that had just arrived. Today was sweaty for a change. Moisture collected in the hollows of my knees and in my armpits, and began to trickle down. Dark sweat patches under my arms were embarrassing, but not half as embarrassing as what had happened the previous week.

Last Wednesday I had started out for work on my bicycle as always. The day looked clear and sunny. But about five kilometres before the theme park in Naantali, the sky went dark, and I realized it was going to start raining soon. I pedalled as fast as I could to try and beat the rain, but the sky tore open just as I was riding down a long stretch with no place to take cover. The rain poured down on me like a shower. In an instant the bike path was a river, and I was soaked through. I could barely see in front of me. Then the cloudburst ended just as suddenly as it had begun. It had done its work and left.

Not until I arrived at work did I realize that soaked through really meant soaked through. I squeezed the water out of my hair and tried to wring my socks dry. For once it felt good to trade my own wet, heavy clothes for the Mymble costume. My underwear was soaked too, but I couldn't do anything about that. I thought no one would notice under the loose outfit.

Mistake.

The front of the Mymble costume instantly stuck to my bra, and lewd wet splotches formed on the fabric around my breasts. That wouldn't have mattered if I could have stayed in the stockroom until the splotches dried, but that day happened to be unusually busy, and I had to stand at the till. Of course every customer's eyes instantly went to my chest, but I just smiled bravely and did my best cheerful customer-service routine. A few young fathers did make comments about my interesting clothing choice, to which I responded by saying something vague about a rainstorm. I wished I could sink behind the counter and disappear. The costume took an excruciatingly long time to dry.

Now I could laugh about it, though. I held two Moomin balls in front of my breasts in the stockroom and thought about organizing a Miss Wet Mymble Costume competition – they had wet T-shirt contests after all. Brushing the shipping dust off the balls, I arranged them in their place. One of these days we needed to do a proper inventory, if we could just find the time. Otherwise at the end of the summer we would have piles of excess inventory because no one could find the right box in all this chaos.

I sat down for a moment on a small stool and listened to the noise on the other side of the door out in the shop. The shrill screams of children, the lilting accents of the Swedish tourists, the grunts of the parents frazzled by the heat. I didn't particularly like my job, but it wasn't unpleasant either. I hadn't developed much of a friendship with any of my co-workers, but they were agreeable enough.

There was a special feeling of freedom and detachment in this summer and this job. I wasn't firmly tied to anything or anyone. I handled my work and was just sociable enough, but no one expected anything more of me. I didn't expect anything more of myself either.

Summer was languor and lethargy. My studies weren't progressing, and none of my relationships were going anywhere. In a way

I enjoyed it. I knew that in the autumn life would tumble forward again in a constant roller-coaster of obligations. School would start, student-union activities would start. There would be parties, vague social expectations, complicated emotions, passionate kisses in dark corners of bars, mornings when it would be hard to look the other person in the eye, friendships on the rocks, difficulty reconciling the past and present, joy and sorrow, stress and happiness. I already longed for it, but at the same time I kind of wished this boring summer could go on for ever.

I got the toy balls unpacked, cut the tape on the cardboard box and took it out to the roller cart outside. After returning to the stockroom, I enjoyed another moment of solitude. Soon I would have to go back out into the shop to be at everyone's disposal, to answer questions, to help, to accept cards and money, to smile, to straighten collars in passing.

But for this one moment I could be alone. Distant. Close. Not quite arrived.

A voice snapped me out of my reverie. It was familiar but also strange. I hadn't heard it for years. Did I hear right? Was it?...

I opened the stockroom door and stepped out into the clamour and heat of the shop. Yes, I had heard right. It was Mariia.

She was with a group of friends, and they were focused on the key-chain display, so she didn't notice me. She looked the same as she had before. Or no, not quite the same. Her long red hair was down, and she had a bit of a tan. She was wearing a white, sleeveless shirt and linen trousers. Her voice was just as loud, her gestures just as animated. And her laugh was just as irritating and irresistible.

I froze in place. My neck burned. My legs were numb and weak, and my hands trembled. What would I say if she noticed me? I would have to say something.

Hi, you might not remember me, but we went to high school together. Although of course Mariia would remember. She had to remember. We had spent two years walking the same halls and stairways, sitting in the same classes at different times. Mariia was a year older than me, and she was my group's peer tutor. We had talked. We had even hung out together, just the two of us, outside of school. Although not as often as I would have liked.

I was already taking a step towards her, but then I couldn't.

I turned around and went back to the stockroom. I leant my back against the wall and tried to calm my pulse. I thought about what I would say to her. All the things I wanted to say.

Hey, I haven't seen you for ever. How are you? I'm fine. I haven't thought of you in a long time.

Why am I telling you this? Because there were times when I didn't do much but think about you. At night I dreamt about you, and during the day I watched for you at school. I couldn't rest unless I caught at least a glimpse of you. It was like a fever, a fog, hypnosis. I couldn't concentrate on anything but you. Friends would talk to me, but I would barely hear them. Nothing else interested me. Nothing but you.

You could say you were my first love. There had been some infatuations before, but I fell in love with you as desperately as only a sixteen-year-old can. I had all the classic symptoms. I lost my appetite. I couldn't sleep. My heart rate rose just thinking about you. When I talked to you, my whole scalp burned, and I felt like an idiot, but I didn't want to be anywhere else. I just wanted to be near you every instant.

Did you ever realize what I felt for you? Did you realize that I was head over heels when I told you my stupid stories too fast and too loud, when I tried to be funny? You must have known something, because sometimes you seemed embarrassed. Or did you just think you were imagining it? You may have wondered about my behaviour, but you still didn't believe it could have been because I was in love with you.

I wanted to save you. It's true. I saw how intense you were about school and everything. You were burning out. Sometimes you looked so small and tired when the others weren't around and you didn't have to put on your usual act. I wanted to soothe you, to take you somewhere quiet and cool and stroke your hair.

That's as far as I thought it through. Or, well, maybe sometimes I imagined kissing you, but that's all. That doesn't mean my feelings weren't strong, though. Back then I just didn't know how to imagine everywhere a kiss could lead. That wasn't the most important part of my love. My feelings for you were innocent and pure. I couldn't feel anything like that any more. I've experienced too much.

With hindsight I've thought about what a strange time those years in high school were. How people in the same school, in the same situations, can live such different lives. Longing for you largely defined my life. It was reflected in everything. School, friendships, hobbies, the things I wrote. When I read what I wrote back then, I realize that in one way or another almost everything dealt with you and my feelings for you. I lived you.

You lived something completely different, though. I realize that now. You had your own wounds and yearnings and sorrows. Which had nothing to do with me. I was only a very small part of your life, barely playing a tiny supporting role. I was that slightly strange girl who followed you around. You were polite and friendly, but I probably bothered you sometimes. When you started dating Lasse, we didn't talk for months. Did you know you'd broken my heart? Could you see in my eyes how much I hurt? Or were you so under the spell of your new relationship that you didn't even notice I couldn't say a word to you any more?

It's strange to think how important you were to me, when I clearly wasn't to you. I'm not blaming you at all. It wasn't your fault I fell in love with you. You didn't do anything wrong; you didn't lead me on. Sometimes this dizzying feeling comes over me when I think that maybe I was important in the same way for someone else whom I didn't really notice. How could I have noticed when I was so stuck on you?

I remember you saying once that you don't like your name. Mariia. That it's difficult and it has one too many Is. That you intended to change it to Maria. I thought it was the most beautiful name in the world. I repeated it to myself quietly at night, mentally caressing that long i sound. Mariia. Mariia.

Even though years have passed and I've experienced big emotions towards other people in a completely different way since then, I can't help but wonder what you felt for me then. Was I a friend? A nuisance? A distraction? Back then I over-interpreted every glance, fancying that they all meant something. But was it all over-interpretation and fancy? Do I even want to know? Will part of me permanently break and disappear if I finally get an answer from you? Will I lose my grasp on the bittersweet fantasy I still cling to? For two years you were the most important thing in the world for me. Would that all flatten into an embarrassing, meaningless nothing?

Why are my hands shaking, and why do I feel like a sixteen-year-old again? I should at least be able to say hello to you like a normal person. I should be able to say... What?

I stared at the ceiling of the stockroom and decided to take a chance. I would walk out into the shop and say hello. I wouldn't think too hard about what I would say or how she would reply. You don't have to know everything in advance.

Just as I came out of the stockroom, the bell on the front door jangled. Mariia and her friends were gone. I started as if waking from a dream.

'What's up with you?' Ella asked. 'You aren't feeling sick, are you?'

'No,' I said, and gradually my hands stopped shaking. 'I'm fine.' That was both true and false.

Slowly I walked over to the key-chain display and started organizing them, even though they already hung in neat rows. For a moment my fingers stopped to stroke a silver Little My figurine.

Then I tugged my collar back into place.

Translated from the Finnish by Owen Witesman

Illustrations by Britta Teckentrup

Mediterranean Cruise

Cathy Clement

August 2016 – my first 'Cast off!' was meant to be a really special moment for me. I'd hoped to stand on deck twelve, right at the top of the boat, bun untied, hair tousled by the wind, soul filled with the indescribably precious sensation of freedom and completeness, all thoughts, random or otherwise, dispelled from my brain by big gusts of wind.

But as is the case in life time and time again – which is to say that things never turn out quite the way you envisioned – I ended up sleeping through my first 'Cast off!' moment.

After the distress-at-sea drill at 9 p.m., I was exhausted and went back to my bunk on Deck Five for a lie-down in the extremely comfy bed beside my son Benjamin. The bed had the same sheets as the ones we have in the hospital. Deck Five is near the lifeboats (specially selected, of course: who hasn't seen *Titanic*?).

Benjamin watched a film about cursed pirates – you know the one I mean. He missed none of it: the farewell melody, the boat hopping around, the captain addressing the passengers, the ship setting sail from the port of Palma de Mallorca. First stop: Côte d'Azur.

I'd only wanted to lie down for half an hour, but ended up sleeping until five in the morning, without waking up once in between.

I guess that was actually a perfect start to the holiday, come to think of it, especially since the weeks leading up to it had been particularly stressful. Besides, I'd had concerns before the trip that I wouldn't be able to sleep when the boat was moving. Or that I'd get panic attacks, being 'alone' at night in the middle of the Mediterranean. I'd worried far too much, as usual. That's the way I am. I had a range of anti-puke tablets with me as well as some valerian relaxant tablets. And a whole host of other medicines, bandages and ointments. Completely unrelaxed.

I often find myself worrying about trivial things. It's only because I don't have any real problems. But just because I can worry doesn't mean I should. Because from an ethical and moral point of view, I'm an idiot.

Hundreds of thousands of rich people go on cruises on enormous luxury liners.

Hundreds of thousands of poor people cross the Mediterranean in small fishing boats, with their children, grandchildren, babies… Hardly any of them can swim. The Mediterranean has become a cemetery, and these people are still squeezing themselves into tatty boats and paying through the nose for the privilege.

I'm ashamed of all of my inane fears and made-up concerns. I really am sorry.

It would be great if I could simply set my head to 'mute' sometimes. I'd be able to enjoy life so much more and wouldn't have as many doubts. I'd be more appreciative in general. There are so many wonderful places in the world to discover, so many great moments that haven't yet been lived; there's still so much out there for me, if only I could allow it. I'm a lucky beggar really. A pessimistic lucky beggar.

According to Info TV, the sun was meant to rise at 6.19 on our first morning at sea. We didn't miss that.

With a handful of fellow passengers, all still half-asleep, we stood right at the top at the bow of the ship and travelled towards the rising sun.

I thought – well, I certainly hoped – that an indescribable feeling of happiness would wash over me at that point, the way it used to whenever I felt the sun on my skin. That my whole body would start to tingle and the feeling of happiness in my tummy, more or less in my solar plexus, would spread throughout my body and take my breath away for a brief moment. With a sigh, I'd feel good, just the way I was.

But that feeling of happiness didn't wash over me that first morning on the boat. It didn't wash over me at all that first day at sea.

What amused us most was the way there were sick bags hanging up all over the place. For a boat like ours, which was almost entirely carpeted, it certainly wasn't a bad investment. The ginger tablets we'd taken had a preventative effect and seemed to work well, despite the choppiness of the sea. It wasn't possible to read by the pool, as everything was constantly blowing around all over the place: towels, plastic cups, children, toys and all. A really breezy experience. No one was badly injured. Amusing, the lot of it.

Day 2: Villefranche-sur-Mer – 6 km to Nice. To the shore by tender boat, followed by a bus transfer.

I spent a lot of time thinking about my younger sister, who, as a ten-year-old girl with blond curly hair and a cheerful, infectious smile, flew on her own from Luxembourg-Findel to Nice like a much bigger girl, without batting an eyelid. With a small rucksack on her back, a name tag around her neck and a white Luxair cap to protect her from the sun. I certainly wouldn't have dared to do it. But she›s a strong person; I admire her.

That's my first personal connection to Nice. Now I'm here I want to wish her *everything* she needs, and hope from the very bottom of my heart, if she's reading this, that everything's going well for her again, and that she can go on a cruise too. I hope she has wonderful feelings of happiness that are so strong that she feels as if she's going to burst with joy.

Later, sometime around 2006, we were meant to be flying to Nice; my youngest son was only two at the time. We didn't go. Benjamin had a really bad cold.

I've had a quick look around Nice now. I wandered along the Promenade des Anglais and didn't discover anything shocking. I thought I'd see something, find something that would remind me of those awful events on the night of the French national holiday. But there were no longer any traces of that horrific massacre. Nice was beautiful. The sun was shining in the blue sky, the sea was so clean that you could see the tiny glittering fish and the round stones when you swam in it. The water was gorgeous and I had a real holiday feeling. However, that deep feeling of happiness – let's call it *Pimpampel*, an old Luxembourgish word for butterfly – unfortunately didn't come. It was as if I couldn't find the gearstick. At the same time, I wanted it so badly.

Apart from a large black plaque on the façade of a building, the side of Nice I encountered seemed untroubled. '*Nous sommes NICE.*' The words had been chosen really well. They're simple and say it *all*. We are *people*.

In the church at the Port of Nice, we lit candles and picked up an extract of the gospel. I'm a practising Christian. I hope it doesn't bother anyone that I stand by my faith. Should I delete that part? No, it's staying.

The Basilica of Notre-Dame du Port is sombre, more what you'd expect of a French church in a small village. The riches of the world can't be found here, that much is evident. But you can find the riches of the soul, modesty and charity, God's protecting hands and many '*Alerte Attentat*' signs pointing you to an app for your phone so that, if you're lucky, you can escape an assassination. If maniacs were to storm a church in an attempt to decapitate the priest, for instance. I think I'm going to throw up.

I don't want to have to think about all of that. To have to explain the unexplainable to my children.

I ended up avoiding the big flea market in Nice, unfortunately. We went round the outside of it. For safety reasons.

But it's precisely those dark, narrow alleys with their tall, old houses providing shade that give cities like Nice their charm. Too much hustle and bustle, too many people. Brave people. Who don't go and lock themselves inside their own four walls to await the next horror story. All the dawdlers and bargain-hunters were living their lives to the full, at their leisure.

What I personally like most are those movable washing lines, hanging out of windows, crossing from one side of the alley to the other, or strung along building façades. Could I live like that?

I'm a different person when I'm in the south of France. The way I used to be. Fourteen again, when I went there with Granny Bertha. My enthusiasm for the south of France will probably never wane.

The summers I spent in Ardèche are some of my most wonderful childhood memories. I was a different girl there to the one I was at home, thanks to my grandmother's unconditional love. I never got into trouble or was made to feel guilty about all kinds of wrongdoings, because I could do no wrong in Grandma Bertha's eyes. For me, she was and is the embodiment of a kind-hearted and loving person. Since converting, I've seen her as more and more of an example, and I'm always pleased when relatives tell me how much I remind them of her. It's a good job I now believe in heaven and guardian angels, because she's watching over me from above and that helps me relax.

I spent the summer holidays at her house when I was fourteen, and she ended up with an expensive phone bill come September because I'd called a sex line four times and listened through to the end of the recorded story each time.

Granny Bertha asked me if I knew how expensive it was. I was shocked and embarrassed, so denied it just to be on the safe side. She then said softly, 'No one has to find out about it now, but please don't do it again, my love.'

Yes, she really said 'my love' and it never was mentioned again. That's what she was like. I'm absolutely convinced that many young people lack love, above all. Unconditional love.

And unfortunately, as a mother myself now, I have to admit how difficult it is to love your teenage children when they're acting as if love within the family were worse than all the infectious diseases put together.

But back to the ship now. I keep digressing.

That kept happening on board too. My thoughts kept jumping from one thing to the next and it was extremely difficult for me to reach a state of inner peace. The completely imperfect exterior of my body was lying naked and motionless on a comfortable lounger in the nudist area on Deck Twelve. And the wildest thoughts were haunting my head. From fear, self-doubt and worry to sadness and pessimism.

'The devil told you that!' screams the crazy imp-like creature in that fairy tale – what's it called again, the one that ends up tearing off its own leg out of self-hatred? Oh yes, Rumpelstiltskin. That's the one.

Example of jealousy: next to me, couples, young and sexy or older and rich, were sunning themselves. Most of the women barely looked their age. They'd taken steps to make sure of it. Many of them had extremely plump breasts, which even looked quite good on some of them. Several were actually wearing make-up at the pool – or was it permanent make-up? The women rubbed sun cream into their husbands' bodies, the husbands ordered cocktails from the pool bar, they read and laughed together, held hands. Yeah, most of them seemed really happy and satisfied.

And I lay there feeling like a jealous, clumsy oaf.

I'm not fat, nor am I particularly repulsive to look at, but the women there by the pool were in a completely different league. What bothered me most, however, was how relaxed they all were, how carefree. It annoyed me so much because I knew that all of my worries were self-inflicted and that I wasn't making the most of the chances I had. I could make so much more of myself, enjoy life so much more, if I only let myself. Aha!

I was jealous of the carefree aura that others gave off. And, once again, I'd discovered another lovable?!?! (grrrr…) character trait of mine. What a compassionate, Christian person I am… oh dear, I've still got a long way to go. Best get started, then!

On the day trips I found it easier not to brood. We went to Pisa next. That was day three. The bus journey through Tuscany was long, but the tour guide talked non-stop the whole way, as if she'd worked in teleshopping or as a football commentator – or whatever

you call it? – in the past. Most of what she said was boring. Still, she repeated it time and time again. Fine.

The thing is, these organized excursions are a bit odd anyway. Somehow they're not quite my cup of tea. Too many plans, too many times, rushing around; no thanks, if I were to go on another cruise, I'd do it differently.

We spent day 4 in Rome.

The funniest part was our small, chubby, peroxide-blonde tour guide Alessandra. She'd converted a red mop into a selfie stick and we had to follow her around the whole day. Via an in-ear receiver, we were linked up to her extremely unusual voice. The best part was that whenever she received a phone call, she'd start ranting in Italian before remembering to cut the connection to the group. Someone really seemed to want to drive her up the wall. In any case, she was temperamental.

Our lunch in a small Roman trattoria was excellent, and I especially liked the lasagne we were served as a starter. We had red wine to go with it, and everything was very relaxed after that. The group grew closer and people spoke and laughed more.

Most of us had taken out our in-ear receivers by then, but that didn't seem to bother Alessandra at all. She still did her best. I didn't envy her having to do that job. Having to speak virtually without pausing for eight hours in a row, day in, day out. She explained that she'd studied art history. She did know a great deal too, with all the dates and everything – there's no way I could remember all that.

Virtually the only thing I can still remember is that the letters in St Peter's Basilica are two metres tall, which you don't realize when you're there because everything is so unbelievably huge, and that 'the yellow thing', as Alexandria called it, right at the top above the altar is the Holy Ghost. In person.

I went, very deliberately, through the Holy Door of Mercy, knowing that all of your sins are then forgiven, but unfortunately I have more vices than hairs on my head. It's a good idea, but simply walking through a door is probably not suddenly going to transform me into a better person.

It's always great after Confession, when you feel that all of your mistakes have been forgiven, but since we people are so fallible, it doesn't usually last very long and we make new mistakes again. For example in the car, when someone inconsiderately pulls out in front of you and you swear at them. Whoosh, that's all it takes.

There's a whole host of mistakes I make on an almost daily basis, but I'd still like to stay compassionate, including towards myself. 2016 is the Year of Mercy, after all.

I bought a small Divine Mercy medal for my car, which I still need to put up. It's meant to remind me not to swear so much when I get stuck in traffic. The car needs to be cleaned first. Clean it first, then make good resolutions. Get rid of the old baggage first.

I learnt a lot on this small journey, thought a lot and, despite everything, also managed to relax and enjoy myself. I sometimes had a good laugh too, together with Benjamin, and that was great!

On the last night in Sardinia, I ripped all of the pages out of my diary. Pages full of worries, fears and concerns. But also containing prayers and glimmers of hope. I ripped it all out and threw it in the sea. A new start. That's the plan.

Incidentally, *Pimpampel* finally showed up. And, as unbelievable as it might sound, it was in the taxi on the way from the ship to the airport in Palma. The old driver, a real romantic, explained how he only ever listened to love songs.

When 'I Swear' came on the radio, a wave of thankfulness and love swept over me. I took in the blue sky, La Seu Cathedral, all the small yachts, my happy, sun-kissed son.

I took in all of that and much more and felt absolutely perfectly happy.

And full of joyful anticipation about HOME.

Translated from the German by Alice Tetley-Paul

Illustrations by Isol

Journey at Dusk

Sandrine Kao

Suitcase-on-wheels; backpack; handbag; oboe.

Blanche ticks off her bags. She must not forget one, no way. She must stay focused, despite her exhaustion from endless hours on a plane.

Her ears are still buzzing from the throb of the plane's turbines, the snores of the man in the next seat and the crackle of the loudspeakers announcing departures, arrivals, delays and changes of departure gate.

Blanche sighs. She needs silence.

She hugs her instrument case tightly and walks swiftly down the long corridor that leads to the arrivals hall, where her aunt should be waiting for her: the aunt she has never met, who must put her up for the whole month.

The squeaking of her suitcase wheels on the lino stops.

Blanche looks up, trying to spot a face she might recognize among the small crowd here to meet the travellers. A middle-aged man waits, his arms folded; a baby in a sling, legs dangling, is rocked by his mother; two children run between suitcases; a family wave their arms frantically at a passenger. Black hair, dark complexions, powder-blushed cheeks, red mouths, up-dos with not a hair out of place, hats, frayed jackets, smart suits…

Blanche scans the group.

Her eyes rest on a woman holding hands with a little boy aged three or four. The woman seems to be looking at her and waving wildly in her direction. Is that her aunt, gesticulating like that?

Surely not. But the woman yells:

'Ban-chi! Ban-chi!'

'Blanche,' she says, correcting her, with a tinge of annoyance.

The grating of her suitcase wheels starts again, but it is soon lost in a stream of words that Blanche barely understands. The woman – whom Blanche may call 'Aunt Mi-i' – has come to get her instead of her aunt, because of a last-minute hitch – she wasn't sure what – but (unlike Blanche) she is delighted they have met.

'Ya ya ya ya,' the small boy pipes up, getting louder and louder, rocking from left to right.

'Give me one of your bags,' signals Aunt Mi-i, seizing the rectangular pouch she is holding.

Blanche shakes her head and clasps the case tightly.

No way will she let her have her oboe!

She is already afraid that the tropical climate will damage the wood of the instrument – she is not going to risk someone carelessly knocking it around as well.

Blanche thinks about the grade exam in the new school year that she must prepare for, which meant she had to bring her sheet music and oboe. She does not want to fail. She would have preferred not to go away this summer, so that she could work. Or rather, just to go for a week, as planned, to Lozère, camping and hiking in the Cévennes mountains with friends. She and her best friend Aurélie would have hatched a plan to get Romain to notice her. She might even have shared a kiss with him, who knows? Instead of which, her parents had the great idea of returning to their country, this very summer, which they hadn't set foot in fifteen years… and to send Blanche on ahead, supposedly to manage by herself a bit and get a handle on the language.

Her parents' country: *meh*. That was how thrilled she was. A load of old ruins left by the war, suffocating heat and homes with dodgy hygiene.

'Stop, come back here!' Aunt Mi-i suddenly yells at the little boy.

He has freed his hand from her firm grip and is charging towards the exit. Aunt Mi-i forgets the case and rushes after the child. She gestures to Blanche to follow.

Suitcase-on-wheels; backpack; handbag; oboe.

Time for the wheels to start their squeaking again. The airport's sliding doors open to let them pass, letting in a wave of hot air and a barrage of indistinct sounds, all mixed up with the noises from the street.

The sky is a dark, purplish blue. It won't be long till nightfall.

Blanche is sweltering. She's dying to jump in a car and get there. But there is no car. Just a bus stop with a vehicle already parked, which Aunt Mi-i hurriedly flags down. She grabs Blanche, who jumps on to the bus.

Backpack; handbag; oboe. The suitcase-on-wheels only just makes it through the door before it closes.

'Yaaaaaaaaa…' warbles the little boy, at length.

He climbs on Blanche's suitcase; she tries to stop him.

'Brat,' she thinks to herself.

The vehicle moves off, toppling the child over; he starts crying and scowling at her, as if it were her fault.

Aunt Mi-i pats him down, dusts him off, stands him up, then goes into tourist guide mode, explaining landmarks as they pass by the windows.

'Over there, that's Peace Avenue. Its name was changed after the fall of the dictator; the highway was named after him before that. And here, this is the memorial to commemorate the people's revolt and honour the victims who perished under army fire. Over there is the royal citadel; it was restored after the war and turned into a museum.'

The monuments fade into the dark blue mass of the sky.

Blanche has a rough idea of the history of the country, so she understands what Aunt Mi-i is telling her, but she does not reply. Blanche can't string three words together in her companion's language.

Her parents ran away from the war after an armed group took power. Along with thousands of other refugees, they tried to reach Europe and were stopped in France. Then she was born and they were able to stay. Her mother had explained to her how difficult it had been to integrate. They had kept a low profile. They had found work, ignored the insults and blended in with the French. As for their country, they didn't speak about it any more.

So Blanche had grown up like any other child, shrugging her shoulders when people pointed out her foreign background. She took refuge in music, that language with no borders, which she loved to speak through her oboe.

It was her father who had given her the taste for music and encouraged her.

'Stop! We're getting off!'

Aunt Mi-i's voice interrupts her musing.

'You absolutely must see the night market and we must stop and eat there.'

Blanche sighs. Her stomach is still churning from the pre-packed food she gulped down on the plane. 'But when will we get there? I want to put my bags down!'

Blanche fights her way through the people.

The roller case trips passers-by.

The backpack catches on funny-shaped fruit on the stalls.

The oboe case handles are dripping with sweat from her hands.

And her remaining bag slips off her shoulder.

Blanche groans with irritation. But at the same time, she recognizes some foods: tropical fruit that she's hardly ever tasted; fragrant delicacies her mother prepared on special occasions. She is thirsty; she wants to bite into a fruit.

The small boy stamps his feet. His little hand clasps a fruit on a stall.

'Don't you help yourself! Mi-i's going to buy some.'

She pays for a bag of fruit. She gives one to the child, another to Blanche.

Blanche bites into it. It's sweet, juicy, refreshing. She wants to say thank you. But Aunt Mi-i has already turned her back. She is collecting another bag from the next stall.

A familiar smell tickles her nostrils: little filled buns, cooking in a large barrel. Blanche is reminded of standing at the stove with her mother, a few years ago.

'You cook bread in the oven!' Blanche had said.

'Not these, you don't,' her mother retorted. 'Here, taste.'

'It's white and soft. And what is that brown stuff inside it? Yuck…'

Blanche had hurt her mother's feelings. Actually, she hadn't found it at all bad: quite the opposite. She had just been a bit fixed in her ideas. But then cooking did not interest her. She was uncomfortable in her own skin, did not know what she ought to love or hate; she followed her friends' tastes, to fit in.

Would Aurélie have liked those little, salty, brioche-style rolls? Very probably not. Aurélie has never asked about Blanche's background. She's never been able to point to Blanche's country on a map.

Blanche sits down. Bag, pack, oboe, all propped against her.

She cradles the little brioche and blows on it, to cool its centre.

'Have you tasted them before? Everyone eats them here, it's the poor person's meal; you can get a roll for a penny. During the war, they made them with no filling.'

Next to her, the child has already swallowed his whole roll in a few mouthfuls. He demands a second.

'No, otherwise you won't eat your dinner tonight.'

'Ya ya yaaa,' the kid scowls, his voice getting more and more insistent. 'Yaaaaaaa!' he's bellowing now.

Blanche tries to ignore the screams jarring her right eardrum.

She bites into the bun and rediscovers the taste of that spice on the roof of her mouth, the same as in her mother's rolls.

She would have liked to go back and ask the name of that spice, the one with such a subtle flavour.

'When she joins me, with Dad, I'll ask her,' she promises herself.

Blanche remembers the only things her parents managed to keep after their exile. They all had that light fragrance, that slightly woody yet sea-salty taste, which means so much here.

A few clothes, which they had never worn again; papers; books; a photo album; two or three pieces of jewellery and that traditional musical instrument her father used to play.

That slight hint of spice: she had tasted it on her tongue when she put the strange flute with eight holes in her mouth, one day when her parents were out. Her father had forbidden her to touch it: he said she was still too little to play with it.

Blanche recollected how she was drawn to the short, wooden cylinder, which didn't seem so fragile to her anyway.

Her mother had told her that her father was a musician before they took refuge in France.

'Whenever he started playing again, I would start crying. When you were in my tummy, you would stop kicking when you heard him.'

But Blanche had no memory of hearing her father play. She did not think of him as a musician. He was a stock-controller in a ware-house. And her mother was a dinner lady. Blanche was ashamed of her parents; Aurélie's were a lawyer and a journalist.

Blanche had seized that moment alone to try to produce a note, but no matter how hard she blew, the air she puffed through the pipe did not produce a sound. She did not know where to put her lips to get it to work. Frustrated, she had set the instrument aside and eventually forgot about it. And when she had discovered Western instruments at music school, especially when she was introduced to the oboe, she had been captivated straight away by its sweet, charming sound, with its slight nasal twang. She enjoyed feeling the reed vibrate on her lips. She would let her fingers run over the keys and vary her technique, making the instrument play a fuller sound when she was feeling melancholy or a more powerful sound when she was angry. Her oboe was her secret lover, her friend, her confidant, much more valuable and precious than any feelings she might have for a boy her own age, even if it was Romain. She never talked about music with her classmates anyhow. She preferred her private chats with her oboe, or conversations with the rest of the orchestra, tuning her 'A' beside the clarinet and the bassoon.

Blanche finishes her roll. She looks around. The kid is opening the bag where her oboe is stowed.

'Oh!' he cries.

Blanche is about to scold him but thinks better of it: it is the first time the child has let out a different sound from his perpetual 'Ya ya's; he seems truly enthralled to find the instrument in its case. He is actually looking at her with big dazzled eyes and doesn't dare touch.

Blanche grants the child her first smile.

She whispers 'shush' very softly to him and closes the zip of the case.

The boy jumps straight up: he pulls Blanche by the sleeve and tries to drag her farther away.

'Where do you want to go?' asks Aunt Mi-i.

The child points to a little square behind the trees and motions to them to listen.

Blanche listens too.

Suitcase; bags; oboe…

Blanche gets up and follows the boy. A melody begins to stand out from the surrounding noises.

Blanche listens carefully to the surrounding sound; she tunes out the cacophony of the cars, the sputtering of the scooters, the crackling of radios broadcasting pop... and finally seizes on the mellow tone of a wind instrument.

The group approaches the square. Great banyan trees spread over it. At last, the noises of the street fade and the only sounds are the lapping of a stream passing close by and the smooth solo of a little wooden flute.

The musician is playing beneath one of the great trees.

Blanche gets even closer. She leaves her bags behind.

At last she sees the instrument close up. A traditional tune is escaping from it, which she almost feels she recognizes: the flute is identical to her father's...

Blanche takes a big breath in and struggles against a tide of emotion.

The man doesn't blow straight into the instrument the way she had tried to do years before: he blows into a reed, a double one, those two strips vibrating against each other, attached to one end of the instrument to produce a sound.

Just like her oboe.

Blanche understands.

Her father's flute no longer had a reed.

It had been lost. On the road to exile, no doubt.

During her parents' journey from this place to France.

So her father had never played his instrument again, because without a reed it could not resonate. Perhaps he'd considered replacing it, getting himself a new one, and then time had passed and he never got around to it.

Beneath his banyan tree, the musician has stopped playing.

Blanche looks around her, admires the shade of the great trees, breathes the air, heavy with humidity and a blend of scents. Night has fallen; a thousand little lights shine out from the blue-black blanket of the sky. The sun sets much earlier here than in France.

'Ya!'

The little boy has picked a flower and brings it to Blanche. She smiles at him. Aunt Mi-i does too.

'Come on Ban-chi,' she says. 'It's time to meet your aunt and put your bags down. She doesn't live very far from here.'

'Blanche. My name is Blanche.'

'Ban-cheu,' the boy repeats, laughing.

She laughs. She will have all the time in the world to repeat to him who she is, all the time in the world to know who she is herself, who they are. She picks up her bags again one last time, the suitcase, the oboe, tucks the flower under her arm and falls into step with Aunt Mi-i, who is humming the last tune they heard under the banyan trees.

Translated from the French by Dina Leifer

Illustrations by the author

Passengers

Inna Manakhova

Bright sunbeams streaked the green walls of the airy train compartment, and a warm summer breeze, which had come in through the welcoming open window, played cheerfully with the striped curtains. A lone boy sat inside, relishing his complete solitude for the past two stops. He stared out the window, completely absorbed, his chin propped on his hand. The train passed endless flowering meadows and fruit orchards, as if travelling through paradise. Beyond them, the boy knew, was the sea – something he had never seen in his life. On the table next to him lay an open book, where the boy had read, 'Life is a remarkable journey in pursuit of one's dreams and the constant anticipation of happiness.' These words really spoke to him and now he silently savoured them, as if they were a hard candy, and smiled to himself. Meanwhile the wind hastily turned the pages of the book, as if trying to reach the end of the story before the window closed.

Beside the book lay a pair of glasses with thick lenses – the boy usually took them off when he was engrossed in thought or a daydream, which happened quite often. Next to the glasses was a plate with a cluster of grapes. The boy had bought them at the last stop, but hadn't yet eaten – he knew that if he were to put on his glasses he'd see the sun shining through the berries, reflecting soft lilac specks onto the white rim of the plate. It was so beautiful that the boy thought it best not to eat the grapes until evening. He remembered that somewhere in his backpack he also had fresh tomatoes and some cheese sandwiches. The boy was waiting for the steward to come round with the steaming black tea, always served in large glasses with engraved metal cup holders, so he could set about eating his lunch. The train was gradually slowing down, already approaching the next station, but the tea still hadn't been brought round. Loud voices and laughter drifted in from the neighbouring compartment, whose door was constantly slamming. It was a group of adults celebrating some sort of adult occasion. The steward had got so worn out bringing them one thing after another after another that she'd completely forgotten about the rest of the passengers. Finally the door of the compartment flew open. The boy sat up and quickly put on his glasses, bringing to mind the price of tea and mentally calculating if he'd have enough change left over for something sweet. But it wasn't the steward with her tea tray: instead it was a sullen, lanky teenager with ginger hair. He was wearing a black T-shirt, dirty shorts and huge, poison-green trainers that looked like two crocodiles.

'Compartment number 8?' he asked, his sharp voice cracking. The boy nodded, taken aback. The teenager purposefully stepped into the compartment, shut the door behind him with his foot, flung his bags onto the top bunk and sprawled casually behind the table.

'Yours?' he asked, pointing to the grapes.

'Yes, help yourself,' the boy offered readily, sliding the plate towards the teenager.

The teenager, not wasting any time, helped himself, and soon all that was left of the grapes were the stems.

'Got anything else to chow down on?' he asked, yawning.

'I've got some tomatoes and cheese sarnies,' the boy answered cautiously.

'Get 'em out.' The teenager gave a lazy wave of his hand.

'They'd be better with tea…' said the boy timidly. The teenager gave a tired, almost reluctant sigh, then furrowed his brow and clenched his fists. The boy shuddered, involuntarily shutting his eyes, but instantly opened them upon hearing the teenager hammering on the wall of the compartment with all his might.

'Hey! Steward!'

A few moments later, a sweaty, heavy-set steward appeared in the doorway. Her hat was askew and the foulard round her neck in disarray.

'Why are you yelling?' she screamed at the teenager. 'And banging on the walls? Maybe someone should bang some sense into you!'

'Bring some tea,' retorted the teenager, not looking at the steward. Then he turned to the boy. 'Got any cash?'

The boy blinked a few times and extended his sweaty palm in which he held a few coins.

'We would like two teas, please,' he whispered, barely audibly.

'Maybe you want me to cook you some borscht, too?' the steward yelped. 'The water boiler broke half and hour ago! And suddenly everyone's itching for tea. Well, forget about it. Not happening!' She proudly lifted her chin, causing her lopsided cap to slide down over her left eye.

'Then we want soda,' said the teenager huffily, not the least bit scared of the steward's anger. 'Your fridge, I assume, still works?'

'Oh, you *would* assume,' huffed the steward in annoyance. 'Got to pay first.'

The teenager turned to the boy with an enquiring glance. The boy wanted nothing more than to take his sweaty glasses off again and not see any of this, but he didn't have it in him to resist, so he obediently reached into his bag, where he had more substantial funds.

A few moment later the teenager was sipping soda from a wet, sticky bottle, staring vacantly out of the window, his headphones emanating the dismal howling of yet another popular rock group. One of his feet, shod in green crocodile, lay across the table, rhythmically swaying to the beat of the melody; the other was barefoot, hanging out of the window to 'air out'. The boy had taken refuge in the corner, and was holding his book tight against his chest and staring at the teenager with wide, frightened eyes that looked unnaturally large behind the thick lenses of his glasses. Even the sunbeams had scattered, not daring to approach the spot where, in the deep shadow of the top bunk, sat the sombre, ginger teenager in his black T-shirt, and the friendly breeze had hidden outright behind the striped curtain, trembling there in fright. They rode like this past another station, and then at the following one they were joined by a third passenger: an attractive and cheerful young man in slim, white trousers with a head of thick, gelled-back hair. As soon as the man entered, the compartment filled with the heavy, sickly-sweet aroma of his cologne. The boy sneezed loudly and the teenager scrunched up his nose, giving the man the side-eye and dismissively turning away. Meanwhile, the young man, not in the least affected by the cold welcome, calmly sat on one of the bottom bunks and opened up an elegant bag. He took out a tablet and, with a faint smile, began looking through some photographs. The boy took off his glasses, wiped them thoroughly with a handkerchief, put them back on and carefully stretched out his neck, trying to sneak a peek at the tablet. He was tired of shaking in the corner, tensely watching his ginger companion, and was looking for some entertainment. After seeing that the photos were of sunbathing beauties in bikinis, the boy sighed heavily, blushing, and took off his glasses once more. Nothing interesting – as he'd suspected. Why is it that when people said goodbye to childhood they became so irritable, despondent and boring? Why did they stop reading good books – ones about happiness – and instead start listening to melancholy songs and looking through stupid photos? Why didn't they socialize with anyone? Were the three of them really going to continue not looking at one another and sitting in utter silence all the way to the seaside?

Meanwhile, outside the window it was getting dark. The sky above the meadows had turned turquoise and, in the distance, a gentle pink, like the foam on top of hot cocoa or the iridescent inside of a seashell. The sun became very small, no bigger than a mandarin, then rolled towards the horizon and melted there, leaving in its wake a single, purple cloud, as if a peacock had lost a feather. Soon all the colours faded, like the embers of a dying fire. The teenager, shivering from the cold, reached up and closed the window, and the young man looked out of the compartment's slightly ajar door and asked someone, in a polite and gentle voice, to turn the lights on in the carriage.

The train stopped at the last station before the seaside, and a girl entered the compartment. She looked to be about sixteen, but to the boy she seemed quite grown up. In fact, he became so flustered in her presence that he dropped his glasses and sat rigidly in his corner for some time, staring at the ground. After he'd recovered, he put his glasses back on and began watching the girl out of the corner of his eye. She wasn't very beautiful – she had narrow, squinty eyes, which gave her a wild, boisterous expression, a long, fox-like nose, a big mouth and a whimsical look about her. She was dishevelled – her chequered shirt was missing some buttons, her long, pink skirt had a stain and her socks and trainers were grey with dust.

However, her long fair hair was incredibly beautiful, and even more lovely were her slender, pale arms – which resembled two tender flower stems.

'Good evening, boys!' she greeted everyone happily, putting her valise on the table with a thud. Then she added, in a sweet, insinuating voice, 'Would someone help me up on the top bunk?'

The teenager jumped up, as if stung by a bee, but the girl seemed not to notice his outstretched hand, and instead stared at the young man in white trousers, with an expression of anticipation and goofy admiration. The teenager frowned, but didn't drop his hand, and since the young man continued to scroll through the photos on his tablet with an indifferent smile, the girl had no other choice than to accept the teenager's help. She reluctantly took his hand, picked up her skirt and dextrously climbed onto the top bunk, flashing her scraped-up kneecaps.

'What happened to your knees?' asked the surly teenager, trying to strike up a conversation. 'Rollerblading accident?'

'Curiosity killed the cat,' said the girl with a smile, and then added, implying she didn't wish to discuss it further. 'Give me my valise.'

'Give me a break,' said the teenager scornfully, and turned away.

'Oh, how sensitive we are,' said the girl, exploding into laughter. Then, sighing, she jumped down from the top bunk, shook herself off like a bird ruffling its feathers and sat down at the table. 'I propose a candlelit dinner! I've got a candle and some chocolates – what about you guys?'

'I've got some tomatoes and cheese sarnies!' the boy blurted out unexpectedly, turning a deep red.

'Excellent, kid. Take out everything you've got.'

Over dinner the girl prattled non-stop.

'Where are you going?' she asked the boy.

'To the seaside, where else?' he answered, a bit surprised.

'I'm going to a rock festival!' The girl announced proudly with a wide smile, never taking her eyes off the young man.

'I'm going to the festival too,' the teenager spoke up. But the girl didn't hear him, not even glancing in his direction.

'I was supposed to go with my friends, but those idiots abandoned me! Apparently there wasn't room in the car for a seventh person. So they can fit six but not seven? But I'm tiny,' she added in a funny, high-pitched voice, sticking out her pinkie as proof. 'I could've sat on someone's lap!' She looked deliberately at the young man, as if expecting him immediately to offer her a seat on his lap.

'Or in the boot,' the teenager tried to joke. But no one laughed and he turned away again, gloomy as ever.

'And I'm not just going there for fun,' continued the girl, in a way addressing the boy, but in reality seeing no one but the young man. 'I'm opening for Cat Call!'

'Is that a band?' The teenager smirked. 'I'm surprised anywhere but the pound will have them with a name like that.' Yet again, his words fell on deaf ears.

The girl continued to chit-chat, giggle and flirtatiously eye the young man, who began returning her glances more and more and eventually even put down his tablet. At first he studied her dishevelled hair, her stained skirt and bitten-off nails with a bewildered expression, but was eventually taken by her amusing chatter, her charming, high-pitched laughter – which sounded like someone had dropped a handful of tiny silver bells – and her delightful, childish antics. He began smiling and finally engaged in conversation.

'I don't listen to hard rock,' he said to her. 'I prefer jazz.'

'I could sing to you – I'd rival Ella Fitzgerald,' she said. 'But I never perform without eating an apple first. Boys, you wouldn't happen to have an apple, would you?'

The young man shook his head. The teenager reluctantly got up from his bunk.

'The restaurant car will have one,' he mumbled. 'Hey, munchkin!'

The boy adjusted his glasses. 'Are you talking to me?' he asked in surprise.

'Yeah, you. You're coming with me. Bring cash.'

'Can you believe that guy?' the teenager burst out, disgusted, as soon as they'd walked out of the compartment. 'I know the type – schoolgirls love him, and their mothers too. But what can you even talk to him about? All his brains went into his hairdo! He spent half the day staring at sun-fried beach babes and grinning like an idiot. And he likes jazz? As if! He wouldn't know jazz if it came up and hit him over the head. But he's sitting there, nodding along – like he knows something, like he gets it. You could say anything to a guy like that and he'll play along. But ask him something concrete and he'll just start spewing out these clichés. But who needs brains when you've got white trousers!'

The boy listened, keeping quiet, although he felt very uneasy, as if he'd accidently found out someone's shameful secret. The teenager continued grumbling and bad-mouthing the young man all the way to the restaurant car. As soon as they walked in, they were deafened by a crowd of drunk, noisy adults – they were celebrating again, their heavy glasses clinking dully. A boisterous song filled with prison jargon boomed from the speakers and the floor was covered in spilt soup – its greasy surface glistened. All the apples in the fruit vase seemed small and shrivelled, and the barmaid was taking so long to serve them that the boy's mood plummeted completely. Finally, they bought the apple that looked the most decent.

'How much money you got left?' asked the teenager. 'Enough for some chocolate?'

The boy handed over his last bill, and they bought the girl a chocolate bar with raisins.

They returned in silence – the teenager sulking and chewing on his lip, the boy stealing tentative looks at his companion. And when they returned, the door to compartment number 8 turned out to be locked.

'What the…' said the teenager quietly, turning pale. He shoved the door, but it didn't give, so he began kicking it.

'Stop it! Don't!' begged the boy nervously, grabbing the teenager by the arm. But the teenager shoved him aside in annoyance, turning back to the door in rage.

'Open up!' he roared, kicking the door. 'Open up this instant!'

But as before, no one heard him. In an act of desperation, the teenager punched the door, then immediately recoiled in pain. He stepped back, breathing heavily, covered in sweat. For a few moments there was complete silence from behind the door. Then, after a metallic click, the door slowly opened. The teenager burst into the compartment like a tornado, grabbed the girl – who stood frozen in shock – and pushed her out into the hall, almost knocking down the frightened boy who had just stepped back in through the doorway. He slammed the door shut and turned towards the young man, who was blushing slightly.

'What do you have to say for yourself?' asked the teenager in a threatening tone.

'What's the matter?' asked the young man coldly, attempting to stand. But the teenager shoved him in the chest and stood over him, fists clenched.

'Listen,' the young man babbled nervously. 'You've got it all wrong. She was the one who closed the door! Let's not start a fist fight over some underage piece of ass!'

Both the boy, shaking anxiously and on the brink of tears, and the teenager, red from rage, stood dumbfounded at his words. They looked at the young man with their mouths agape, unable to believe their ears. Suddenly, the teenager's rage was gone, as if erased.

He stood there for a bit, looking the cowering young man up and down with contempt, then spat, with relish, at his own feet. Smirking, he mumbled something inaudible and slowly climbed up onto his bunk. The boy took refuge in the corner, took off his glasses and began silently crying. The door opened once more – it was the girl. She looked inside timidly, but no one paid attention to her any longer. On the contrary, all three, as if on cue, turned away and acted like they were busy doing their own things: the young man focused on his tablet, the teenager put on his headphones, and the boy hid behind his open book. The girl attempted to revive their conversation – voicing something unintelligible and even offering to sing – but got no reaction, so she picked up her valise and, with drooping shoulders, slowly walked out of the compartment and didn't return again. When the carriage lights had been turned off and everyone had finally got into bed, the boy lay motionless for a long while, listening to the beating of his own heart – almost imperceptible over the rumbling of the wheels. Then he got up, rustling like a hedgehog, grabbed the forgotten apple and chocolate bar off the table and quietly slipped out of the compartment into the cold gleam of the hallway, where it was draughty and the wheels clattered all the more. He sneaked along it to the empty, dirty gangway that reeked of cigarette smoke and found the girl standing at an open window. The night wind was playing with her wonderful fair hair, and her valise was on the ground next to her, leaning against her leg like a loyal dog. The girl was looking out of the window and smiling dreamily. The boy looked out too and practically jumped from joy. He was finally seeing it, for the first time: the sea.

Translated from the Russian by Jane Bugaeva

Illustrations by Ole Könnecke

The Longest Pedestrian Route in the World

Laura Gallego

As he did every morning, Hao walked Grandmother Lin to the toilets, where the usual queue was forming, while his mother Yue stood in line for breakfast and his father Qiang went to the office to check the waiting list.

They'd been in the camp for seventeen days now and had yet to be called up. There was only a week left till the registration deadline, and if they didn't reach their destination by then they'd have to go back to their village.

The urban population was controlled by a strict system based on birth and immigration, and only rarely did a special registration period open up. The last one had been sixteen years ago, and there was no telling when the next would be.

They knew it was a slow process, but Grandmother Lin's persistent flu had kept them from coming any sooner. They wouldn't think of travelling without her, because according to the rules families had to register all together, or leave behind anyone unable to come. Fortunately, Grandmother had recovered and they'd arrived before the deadline. Now they were waiting to be allowed to travel before the crossing was closed again.

Hao could see that the system was well organized. The process had drawn millions of people from the rural zones, but given the circumstances it was operating smoothly. New arrivals were placed on a list and housed in tents that were comfortable enough, considering how temporary they were. The food wasn't plentiful, but no one went hungry. There were recreation areas and medical care.

Everything required standing in a queue, but the lines moved quickly. Everyone knew the schedule and the procedures, and that they weren't waiting in vain. Thousands of people made the crossing to the big city every day. You had to wait your turn for weeks at a time, but it would come sooner or later.

They were just returning from the bathrooms when they saw Qiang running nervously toward them.

'We're on today's list!' he announced.

Hao felt a hollowness in his stomach that wasn't hunger. He and Grandmother Lin went to find Yue, while Qiang headed towards the access gate. They ate their breakfasts quickly and set aside a bowl of noodles for Qiang, which Hao ran to take to him.

There was a waiting area with benches, which you could only enter if you were on that day's list. Hao showed his ID to the official, fearing he wouldn't be allowed in, but the man let him go ahead. He searched for his father among the waiting travellers. Qiang saw him first and called out, and Hao went over and handed him his breakfast.

'Where are your mother and Grandmother Lin?'

'They went to get our bags. They'll be here in a minute.'

Qiang nodded. Hao sat down, but it was hard for him to hold still. He looked around to pass the time and noticed a girl hurriedly eating breakfast, like his father. She caught his glance and smiled at him, a noodle still hanging from her mouth. Hao blushed. He was ten years old, and the girl must have been about fourteen; it embarrassed him a little to have caught her attention without meaning to.

He didn't see anyone with her and wondered whether she was travelling alone. It was unusual for minors to cross the pass without an adult, but sometimes it happened.

At last Yue and Grandmother Lin arrived. They all sat on Qiang's bench and waited.

They spent the day in a state of worry, alert to the series of names being called over the loudspeakers. Every three hours the delivery crews distributed food and water. Travellers passed through the access gate at a steady pace, but the room never emptied out, because more people kept arriving.

As evening fell, Yue said, 'It will be night soon. I'm worried we'll have to make the crossing in the dark.'

'There are lights on the road, and the cars will have their head-lamps on.'

'Even so, it will be dangerous.'

'At any rate, it will take us three days to cross to the other side,' Qiang pointed out.

Hao sighed. So it was true. He'd seen the superhighways on TV and knew how enormous they were. People slept overnight on the traffic islands because there was no way to make the crossing on foot in a single day. The international media called it the longest pedestrian route in the world.

Even so, it seemed impossible that it could really exist.

'Everything will be fine,' Qiang reassured them. 'We'll cross over on the pedestrian route and in a few days we'll reach the city.'

It was already getting dark when a voice rang out from the loud-speaker, 'Wei Qiang!'

They leapt to their feet.

'They're calling us,' said Qiang, but Yue held him back: 'Wait. What if it's another Wei Qiang?'

The speaker announced, 'Chen Yue!', then 'Gong Lin! Wei Hao!' 'That's us!' cried Hao.

An official at the gate waved them forward, collected their papers and checked their names against the list, all without a word. Then he stamped their passes and handed them back with the rest of the documents.

They passed through the entrance, where other officials were handing out reflective vests, as well as face masks to protect them from the air pollution. Hao's family took these and put them on.

Naturally, they had to form a queue. It was already completely dark by the time they reached the edge of the highway. The travellers entered the pedestrian route, bathed in the light of vehicles that roared impatiently as if wanting to run them over. Hao started counting the white lines on the ground, but Yue interrupted him:

'Put on your face mask, Wei Hao.'

Embarrassed, the boy obeyed. When he stepped onto the road he was trembling with fear and excitement.

They looked down as they made their way, so as not to be blinded by headlights.

'Keep moving, please,' the guards called out, and, intimidated, they picked up their pace. In theory, they had time to reach the traffic island before the light changed, but it was better not to dawdle.

They walked in silence, breathing through their masks. Soon they reached the island before the klaxon sounded; they had got through the first stretch with no trouble.

This is why it took so long to make the crossing: every two hundred metres they had to stop to let cars go by.

The islands were covered to protect the travellers from inclement weather. There was room to set out chairs or mats, and there were food stalls, but the family felt too restless; they unfolded a chair for Grandmother Lin, then sat down on the ground to wait.

Just before the klaxon sounded again, they gathered at the side of the road behind the safety barrier. Cars were going by so fast that they seemed like blurs of colour wrapped in smoke and gusts of hot air. Then the lights changed again, the vehicles stopped and the travellers continued on their way.

Second island. An hour's wait. Green light. Go.

Third island. An hour's wait. Green light. Go.

They didn't speak; the noise drowned out their words and the smoke irritated their throats in spite of the masks. Grandmother Lin breathed with difficulty, and Hao offered her his arm to lean on.

Then an impatient driver blew his horn right next to them. Grandmother Lin gave a start, tripped and fell to the ground.

Hao rushed to help her, and his parents walked back towards them in alarm, but someone else had already helped Hao and his grandmother before his parents got there. Hao was tongue-tied when he saw that it was the girl who'd been eating noodles. She smiled at him from behind her mask.

Qiang and Yue carried Grandmother Lin away from the car that had honked at them, and Hao and the girl followed.

'Thank you,' he managed to say.

'Not at all! My name is Pan Huiling.'

Hao introduced himself, then asked, 'Are you making the crossing by yourself?' Huiling nodded. 'And did you get to the camp by yourself too?'

'No, my grandmother came with me, then she went home to take care of my grandfather, because he's too old to travel.'

Huiling added that she would live with her aunt and uncle in the city once she was registered. She didn't mention her parents, but said that maybe she'd never see her grandparents again.

'Years ago, anyone could come and go from the cities whenever they wanted. But the cities grew out of control, and the government decided to limit their growth.'

Hao nodded. He'd studied this in school.

'At first they tried fences,' Huiling went on, 'then walls. But those didn't work, and they just slowed down the traffic. So they found a way to solve two problems at once: they built the big modern superhighways. There were roads before, but not with so many lanes.

They made a network that connected the whole country, but the new roads only linked the big cities and ringed them with bypasses. So city people could travel on the highways, but outsiders couldn't get onto them. They're more effective than any wall: thousands of cars driving at 120 kilometres an hour. You can only get through on these pedestrian crossings, and they're guarded very closely. Try any other way and you'll get run over.'

She said all this in a rather ominous tone, as if telling a horror story. Hao shivered.

'Yes, I knew this already,' he answered.

'I figured you did. But it's important to say it out loud, because when you just think it, it seems as though it's always been this way. And it hasn't: there used to be a time when people could travel freely, when the cities were open to everyone.'

Hao looked around uneasily. But the passing cars were making so much noise that no one had heard them.

They met up with the others at the next island. Because of Grandmother Lin's fall, they arrived just when the klaxon sounded. Hao shook when the horde of cars started up just behind him.

They sat down to rest, and Hao introduced Huiling. They welcomed her eagerly when they heard she was travelling alone. The stop was more enjoyable because of her. She made no more gloomy comments about the highways, but cheered them up instead with stories of her stay at the camp. When the klaxon sounded, they all stood up with lighter hearts.

They continued along the crossing until dawn reached them at one of the islands, where they paused to eat breakfast.

By noon the heat was stifling. The sun had cleared away the fog, and at last they could make out enormous buildings on the horizon. But if they turned to look back, they could no longer see the place they'd left the night before.

'We're halfway there,' Qiang announced as they ate their midday meal.

Grandmother Lin let out a small sigh, but she stood up when the klaxon sounded.

So the rest of the day went by, and by nightfall they no longer felt like talking, Huiling's commentaries barely drawing a faint smile. When they stopped for supper, Grandmother Lin, looking overwhelmed, took off her mask to breathe more freely and began to cough. Alarmed, the family tended to her as best they could, and when the coughing subsided, they agreed to stop there for the night, even though this would delay their arrival in the city.

They slept poorly, what with the roar of the cars and the steady murmur of travellers making the crossing. The next day felt even longer than the one before. The city was now very near, but they were much more tired. At night they stopped again but couldn't sleep, so they ended up rising once more and continuing on their way.

Some hours later, Grandmother Lin said that she couldn't go on. Disheartened, they stopped for a rest at the next island.

'Courage!' said a passer-by. 'There are only three more stretches of road to go!'

Hao went to take a look and came back with good news. 'It's true!' he said, 'I can see the access gate in the distance now.'

They continued walking. Hao travelled the last part of the journey as if in a dream, Huiling leapt along beside him, and even Grandmother seemed to walk with a lighter step.

At last they left the road and entered a broad walkway, where officials were gathering people into lines to pass through another access gate.

They hugged each other excitedly and took their places in line, barely paying attention to the klaxon announcing that the light was about to change, or the ferocious roar of the car engines. But then they heard an awful thud, and some shouting, and the honking of horns. They turned around in line as guards wearing grave expressions made their way through the crowd.

'Someone's been hit,' people were muttering. 'What terrible luck, so close to the end.'

'It happens,' Qiang said sadly. 'The crossing is safe, but some people are in such a hurry to reach the other side that they don't pay attention at the final stage. Don't look, Hao. It's not a pleasant sight.'

Hao turned towards Huiling. She was staring intently at the road, where emergency workers were attending to the fallen traveller. Her face was a mask of terror. Hao tried uneasily to get her attention – then Huiling began to scream.

It was very confusing. Hao tried to calm her, but she turned round shrieking, and when the grown-ups held her she started kicking with all her might. At last they managed to settle her down, and a guard approached them. Huiling was trembling and crying, a lost look on her face.

'Did this girl come with you?'

'Yes,' Grandmother Lin answered firmly.

The guard left Huiling in their care. As the line moved forward, Hao and his family tried to get a response from her, but she kept on quietly weeping.

When their turn came, everyone showed their papers. Hao showed Huiling's card, but she stayed expressionless. The official stamped the documents and let them pass. They walked through the checkpoint, leaving behind the pedestrian route it had taken them three days to travel. Hao was dazed, and his parents seemed relieved, but Huiling remained elsewhere, far away.

On the other side there were people waiting for the travellers, carrying welcome gifts or signs with their names. Then Hao noticed a man holding a sign that read, 'Pan Huiling,' and ran towards him, followed by his family. The man introduced himself as Pan Haifeng, Huiling's uncle, and showed photographs of them together, but she only stared with no sign of emotion.

'She's upset because we've witnessed an accident,' Qiang explained. 'But she's a very happy girl. I don't understand why she's taken it so hard.'

Mr Pan nodded sadly. 'When Huiling was small,' he explained, 'her parents tried to make the crossing. She escaped unharmed, but her parents were hit by a car and died. I thought she had no memory of it…'

He told them he'd asked for permission to go meet her on the other side, but the officials were so overwhelmed by the number of applications that the papers had not arrived in time.

'I'm very grateful to you for accompanying her,' he said.

Hao took Huiling's hand to rouse her spirits. She looked at him and finally smiled. So together they went inside the entrance station, leaving behind the enormous highway with its millions of cars, its endless pedestrian route and the sea of travellers still making their way across it in search of a better life.

Translated from the Spanish by Dan Bellm

Illustrations by Barroux

What We've Lost

Sarah Engell

I let go of your hand and lean on the railing as I get to my feet.

'I'll get it,' I say, my voice drier and stranger than ever.

The heat makes everything hazy, the horizon a glassy blur that never gets closer.

I stand in line holding an empty tin can and the lid from a deodorant. The sun burns into my scalp. Every time the boat lurches, someone stumbles. Everything's become so weak. Our legs, our sense of balance, our dreams.

The man who's lost three daughters is pouring the water. A little bit for each of us.

I try my best not to spill any as I stagger back over vomit, rubbish and bodies.

The tin can has the most in it, so you get that.

'Don't be scared, little brother. I'll look after you.'

I smile at you, but you don't see it.

Drops of salty water hit my face and then dry, so it feels like I'm wearing a mask. The waves are higher now. They crash over the railing and push the boat from side to side.

The boy who's lost a brother says it's because there's land nearby. He says it's a good sign.

We'd been on the water for seven hours when the engine packed in. Billowing black smoke, followed by silence. We opened all the cans of fuel and smelt them. Salt water. Just like the water surrounding us.

After the panic, silence descended. Now the sea will decide. I don't know whether we're going in the right direction or back where we came from. I don't know anything. It's as if the darkness has permeated right into my soul.

Someone must have lied to us.

The adults shush me and say I mustn't be afraid. The more they shush me, the more afraid I get.

A big wave breaks against the boat and I lean over you to protect you. I've taken you up onto the prow. Where no one else wants to sit.

We hold hands as I look out into the blue nothingness. The sky, the sea, time. It all blurs together, and I'm starting to feel nauseous, as if I'm only now getting seasick, several days after we first boarded.

At the start there were so many of us we had to sleep sitting up. The sea changed colour around us. From blue-green and dazzling to black streaked with silver. That was how I kept track of time.

But there came a point where I stopped counting the days. I started to close my eyes whenever I heard the loud splashes. I know what they meant.

I'd been so scared of drowning. The wooden boat creaking and the sound of the water so close. But it isn't the sea that kills. It's the burning sun, the hunger and the madness.

One man jumped into the water because he was sure he could see land. One was thrown overboard because he tried to set fire to the boat. It's as if the desperation burrows deep down and makes it impossible to see clearly.

We should have made it ages ago.

Last night I heard some of the men whispering that we're on our last container of water. When it's empty, we'll have nothing.

I lay for a long time staring up at the sky as I clutched your hand in mine.

It's still dark when I'm woken by a baby crying. Crying in panic.

I put a blanket over you and stagger to the stern, where the man who's lost two sisters has already picked up the baby. He cradles and shushes it as he stares out across the sea. His eyes are empty, making my throat tight and dry.

The baby's mother lies on her back with one breast exposed, her eyes no longer seeing. She'd got quieter and quieter since her husband's dead body had been thrown overboard. Now, no matter how hard they try to rouse her, she remains quiet. The baby cries and cries, and the man who's lost two sisters closes his eyes.

I don't know what's happening to me. It's you I'm thinking about when I reach out for the baby and clutch it close to me. I stand on unsteady legs as the boat rolls. Then I kneel down and put the baby on top of its dead mother. Her body is still warm. I help the baby to her breast. It keeps crying, and I'm about to start crying too. Then, finally, it latches on, and as if by some sort of miracle there's still milk. As if her body lives on after she's left it. It's only then I start to cry.

When I lie down next to you again, I can't get to sleep. I keep thinking about the warm baby in my arms. How I got it to sleep. I want to tell you about it, but my throat is too dry. Instead I lie looking at the sky, which is just as deep and dark as the sea beneath us.

It was night when we came aboard and sailed away from everything we knew. We waved in silence. Even those of us who didn't have anyone to wave at.

The only person who didn't wave was you. You were so angry and scared that your little body shook.

I took your hand and lifted it. But you tore it back.

You've always been afraid of water, and I held you and whispered: 'You're the bravest little boy I know.'

By sunrise the sea has calmed again. I stare out over the surface of the water and it's as if the sun is burning fiercer than ever.

Behind me the men's quarrelling has been replaced by silence. The baby has been crying for a long time. There's no more milk in its mother's breast, and I close my eyes when they lift her over the railing. The splash is like a punch in the gut, yet still I look. Her body floats for a moment on the surface. Then it slowly sinks towards the ocean floor.

I stand by the railing and look down into the deep.

The baby is quiet.

From now on it'll be the baby that's lost its parents.

That's how we refer to each other. Not by name, but by what we've lost.

An arm comes around my shoulders. The boy who's lost a brother follows my gaze, down into the darkness, where her body can no longer be seen.

'Their souls will never know peace,' he says. 'They'll roam the sea for eternity. Some of them will look for land. As if continuing the journey.'

'Liar.' My voice is only a whisper.

'Once, when my dad was out fishing, his net got caught and he had to dive down to get it loose. Do you know what he saw?'

'I don't want to know.'

'A human skeleton. It was sitting on the ocean floor like it was at a fancy dinner party. Upright with its mouth open and empty sockets where eyes should have been. Small fish swimming in and out of one of them. It's one of the most horrible things he's ever seen. And he's seen a lot.'

I push his arm away and stumble back to the prow, where you're waiting.

At night I clutch your body close to mine. I put my hands over your ears so you won't hear the water slapping against the boat and the awful silence from the deep.

Above us the sky is so full of stars it seems magical. I've never seen anything so beautiful. I can feel the starlight in my very core.

'Don't be afraid,' I whisper. 'I'll look after you. I promise.'

And while I look up at the sky, I actually believe it.

I must have fallen asleep at some point, because the sound of more quarrelling wakes me up.

'He's taking twice as much water as the rest of us! It's his fault we're all going to die. Let's throw him overboard. Let go of me!'

It takes a while for me to understand they're talking about us. Dizzy with tiredness and panic, I let go of you and stagger down to them. The boy who's lost a brother stares at me.

I stare back.

'What's this? My little brother should go without water? Is that what you're saying?'

He looks away.

'That's what we all say. The others are just too cowardly to say it aloud.'

'Is this true?' I look around, but everyone looks away.

My voice trembles. I feel it even before it leaves my throat.

'He's only seven. How can you be so…' I press my lips together.

The man who's lost three daughters gets up and lays a hand on my head.

'There's hardly any water left. We need to rethink this.'

I push his hand away.

'You can't do this. You can't just decide who's most important.'

'We voted. While you were sleeping.'

The sun burns through my scalp into my thoughts.

'Fine,' I say. 'So I'll give him my water. Better he makes it than me.'

They all watch me when I get my one ration of water and carry it over to you.

'Don't listen to them. It's the hunger and the splashes. Those splashes would drive even the bravest human being crazy.'

They watch me as I press the tin can to your lips and carefully pour the water into your mouth.

They don't understand. They don't understand what it means to love another person more than yourself.

Sometimes I wish the whole boat would sink. Then I would hold on to you and never let go.

The next day we run out of water. The boy who's lost a brother keeps frowning at me, but it's as if everyone's trying to save their energy. People don't even get up to pee.

The stench and the silence shimmer in the air.

The baby that's lost its parents is being breastfed by the woman who's lost one of her twin boys. The twin who is still alive sucks his thumb while the baby eats.

Mum once told me that if a woman breastfeeds another woman's child more than five times, their children become siblings.

Perhaps you also become siblings if you survive something like this together?

The waves are higher again. Every time the boat rolls, you roll too. I lie close to your body and hold you.

'We'll make it,' I whisper. 'We'll be helped ashore, and there'll be no bombs. There'll be no one to hurt us. We'll sit in the shadow of a tree and eat ripe fruit that we picked ourselves. We'll have clean clothes, and there'll be no bombs.'

I don't know how much time passes. It's as if the sea and time are one and the same. As if everything is fluid and we're lying on the wet deck with flies in our nostrils, too exhausted to wave them away. They must have come aboard with us, and now they've taken over the boat. The more prone we lie, the more they buzz and crawl on us.

I try to keep my eyes open, but they keep drooping closed.

We're at a fancy dinner party and my teeth are awash with water, fresh bread, glistening meat kebabs and lavish cakes. Fish swim in and out of our eye sockets, and you laugh because it tickles. Your laughter is just like before. So bright and lovely that it would have brought tears to my eyes if there hadn't already been a whole ocean in there.

One of the fish comes close. One of those ones with a light in front of it. It swims right up to my face and you laugh at how scared I am. I hate the fish. It's too close and the light's too bright. It makes everything else disappear. The cakes, the bread, you.

'Hello?' it says. 'Are you awake?'

I reach out to it and hit something hard and metallic.

A torch.

I sit up abruptly and the sudden movement makes me dizzy. The sea is still dark and there's a big ship alongside our boat.

Our rescuers are wearing white. Like angels, I think, clutching your hand in mine.

We're saved, little brother. We're finally saved.

The relief is a balloon expanding in my chest so I can hardly speak.

The man with the torch extends a hand. I don't take it.

'Help my little brother first,' I say. 'He's only seven.'

The man looks at you.

Looks at me again.

There is a hesitation in his eyes that panics me.

'He's scared of water,' I say. 'Please help him.'

The boat tips every time the angels jump aboard and help people up. Soon all the others are up there and I can't stand the man's reluctance any more.

'You have to understand,' I say. 'He didn't want to come at all. But I convinced him. It was me that convinced him.'

My voice cracks and the man puts a hand on my shoulder.

'There, there,' he says. 'Of course we'll help your brother.' He squeezes my shoulder, which makes me cry.

He switches off the torch and lifts you up from the deck. There are flies in your nose and half-open mouth, and he carries you like a baby. Your arms and legs dangle as he carries you across to the rescue ship.

I only grab the ladder and follow once you're safe.

The man stands waiting for me with you in his arms.

'What will you do with him?' I whisper. 'Don't throw him in the water. Don't leave him to sit on the ocean floor all alone. He's only seven.'

'We won't throw him in the water. Don't fret. It's good you made it. Both of you.'

I lean on the railing and look at your face. The first rays of the morning sun make the sea shine amber, and somewhere behind me I can hear a baby crying. The woman who's lost one of her twin boys carries the baby and the remaining twin, one in the crook of each arm. She catches my eye and gives me a weak smile.

'You're safe now.' I whisper it in your ear as I clutch your hand. 'You're the bravest little boy I know. And now you're safe.'

One of the angels comes over to us. She gives all the survivors biscuits and water.

You're the only one who doesn't get any.

I keep watching you as you're taken away. Your lifeless arms swing back and forth. It looks like you're waving.

Translated from the Danish by Siân Mackie

Illustrations by Joëlle Jolivet

How the Gods Came to Abandon Their Mountain and Go Travelling

Gideon Samson

In the beginning I was never bored. The earth was still fascinating and surprising, and in those days we gods (I'm taking the liberty of speaking for all of us here) enjoyed nothing quite so much as mucking about with people.

We were always wandering down from Olympus, our heavenly mountain, singly or in pairs, to occupy the mortal world below with love and war and stuff like that. We'd disguise ourselves as animals, plants or even humans to avoid being recognized and give ourselves a free hand.

Thanks to all that mucking about of ours – and I don't mean that as disrespectfully as it might sound – stories arose that the people

on earth told and told and told each other so much and so often that there was no way any of them could ever forget us. That, at least, was what we thought.

For a long time things went smoothly. We had it good up on our mountain, with an excellent view out over all those millions of playthings with their little heads and arms and legs, doing all kinds of crazy things that made us gods roar with laughter or weep bitter tears or – when we really couldn't bear it any longer – go down and get involved.

'A little restraint would be nice,' said Hera, my ridiculously jealous better half, and more than once. I'd shown myself amongst mankind again and done a little dancing or something like that with a nice female of the species (by far the most fascinating variety), and somehow or other – don't ask me how – Hera had found out about it in next to no time.

'I am *so* sorry,' I would tell her in situations like that, and often she'd forgive me and that was that. Sometimes, when she felt I really had gone too far, she'd want to take revenge as well, but I understood. It's a woman's right.

For hundreds of years we entertained ourselves with the earth's inhabitants, but eventually almost all games grow dull. I'll be honest: I woke up one morning and couldn't care less.

'I'm bored,' I told Hera.

'Me, too,' she had to admit.

We called the gods together for a meeting (we did that often in those days) and it turned out *everyone* was bored. And not just a little bit! We were sick to death of messing around with people.

'We should just stop!' Hera thundered.

'And that's for you to decide, is it?' I asked, because last time I checked *I* was the thunder god.

She fell silent, hurt, but I couldn't deny she had a point. If we continued occupying ourselves with people, sooner or later, despite our immortality, we would *die* of boredom, and that of course was something we would rather avoid.

'Fine,' I decided. 'From now on we won't meddle with the world. Is that clear?'

There were nods and mumbles of approval.

'That goes for all of us,' I continued. 'Understood?'

Mumbling and nodding.

'It's boring and stupid and, more to the point, we have a lot more fun here on our mountain. We can entertain ourselves without that riff-raff down below. Am I right?'

More nodding and mumbling and then we all agreed that we would leave mankind to it until further notice.

'You mean we'll just let them stew in their own juices?' asked Apollo, a son who'd turned out better than some of the others.

'That's one way of putting it,' I replied. 'End of meeting.'

The years that followed on Olympus were wonderfully relaxing for us gods, but meanwhile, without my noticing – stupid idiot that I was! – little things started changing below us. For centuries upon centuries, our existence had been so self-evident that we simply didn't see what was happening in the world without our involvement. While we were hanging around unsuspectingly on top of our mountain, people stopped telling all those magnificent stories. And that was the start of the Great Forgetting.

First mankind forgot our Olympian adventures, then that everything on earth revolves around us and finally that we even exist. And as if that wasn't bad enough, they started making up totally new gods, gods they feared and served and revered more than they ever had us.

'Father,' said the wise Athena after some half-million days. 'It can't go on like this.'

As it had been a good while since I'd paid any attention at all to events below, I didn't know what she was talking about at first, but when Athena says something it's generally quite sensible – she's my favourite daughter for a reason – so I listened carefully.

'How do you know all this?' I asked when she was finished.

'By looking down,' she admitted.

This confession surprised me, because that was the very thing we had expressly agreed to stop doing.

'Yes, Father, but—'

'It's fine,' I said. 'Don't worry about it.' The seriousness of the matter had already got through to me and I realized that this great forgetting was much more important than my daughter's disobedience. I asked how long it had been going on.

'A while,' she answered.

'We'd better hold another meeting,' I suggested. 'With all of us.'

'When?'

'Immediately.'

For the first time in more than a thousand years we gods gathered again. My characteristically enthusiastic son Dionysus began by handing out metal cylinders and everyone accepted them eagerly.

'Can of Coke?' he asked, passing one to me too, but I had never seen the things before and asked him where he'd got them.

Dionysus looked down contritely and held his tongue.

'You too?' I felt a fury rising within me. 'Doesn't anyone stick to our agreements?'

But even before my son could start on a long list of excuses, I had accidentally fiddled one of those effervescent cans open and took a sip out of curiosity. My anger disappeared like the stars at dawn.

'Good stuff,' I said.

'Sure is!' He sounded relieved.

Then the meeting began and my passionate and invariably wise daughter led us through a discussion of human events we had been blind to for aeons.

'It's gone on too long!' Athena exclaimed.

'I'll drown them all!' bellowed my brother Poseidon, who has always been known as something of a hothead.

'Give us a break,' said Apollo. 'You've already tried that so many times. It never works.'

'What?' Again I was completely in the dark.

'Every now and then he comes up with another flood or a tsunami...' Apollo nodded at Poseidon and shook his head disdainfully. 'But the people build embankments and bridges, and nowadays they've got all kinds of electronic doodads too. In the end they always beat him.'

I thought I was being clever and remarked that at least they hadn't forgotten Poseidon.

'Exactly!' my brother roared, but Apollo shook his head again and explained that mankind invented all those things to control the water alone. Not the gods.

'But we *are* the water!' I cried indignantly.

'You and I know that, Father,' Athena said with a trace of gloom in her voice. 'But on earth they haven't got a clue.'

To be honest I was starting to feel a bit miserable. I'd already twigged that things weren't looking great for us, but it was a blow to realize just how bad they had got.

'I know!' insisted Ares, my most fanatical son, after a few worthless ideas from the others. He sipped his Coke, let rip with a filthy belch and said, 'We'll turn it into one big bloody war and they'll wipe each other out!'

'What a delicious plan!' my daughter Aphrodite cried. Looks rather than brains have always been her long suit, but I have to admit that for a brief moment I too thought that might be the solution.

'A vicious plan, you mean,' Athena corrected her sternly. 'And it makes no sense anyway, because nowadays mankind start wars all by themselves.'

'Really?' I asked. 'Without the gods?'

Surreptitious whispers rose here and there in the meeting hall, and it seemed more and more like I was the only one who *hadn't* looked down in the last few centuries.

'In the name of the gods,' Athena explained. 'Sometimes. But you shouldn't take that all too seriously.'

The meeting was long and tedious. All my brothers, sisters, children, uncles, aunts, nephews, nieces and even a few grandchildren had something to say, but none of them came up with a decent plan that would give our existence on earth a real boost.

At some stage Hephaestus – that ugly, hobbling son of mine – came up with the idea of enveloping the entire globe in a thick layer of flame, but nobody could work out what exactly it was supposed to achieve, so that proposal too was soon voted down.

The breakthrough came from unexpected quarters. After a few hours of pointless discussion, my grandson Pan, who had kept reasonably quiet up till then, suddenly produced a noise that made us all jump.

'Is something wrong, nephew?' Apollo asked.

Pan put down those eternally annoying pipes of his and stood up, wobbling terribly on his hooves and almost giving me a fit of the giggles. He was deadly serious though when he asked, 'Don't you see?'

Nobody understood him.

'It's over,' Pan said. 'Finished, ended, done.' His words were dark, but the voice he was saying them in was anything but. Pan was even smiling as he spoke! 'We're finished here,' he went on. 'Our task is completed.'

It stayed quiet in the hall. Quiet as a mouse. That crazy Pan was standing there with a goatish grin on his face because he *knew* he was right, and we were sitting there dumbstruck, because we knew it too.

OK, I thought, but what do we do about it?

The silence continued. If someone had been listening carefully in that instant they would have heard the creaking of my Olympian brain.

'Father,' Athena said at last, after minutes of futile strain. 'Say something!'

All heads swung towards me like a flock of starlings, and even my wife Hera – who doesn't usually rate me at all – seemed to be looking at me expectantly.

'Me?' I asked.

Nobody said anything. They kept staring at me, and that started making me pretty nervous. Until I realized – you could call it divine inspiration, though that might be overstating it – that only one thing was possible.

'Yes, me,' I said, answering my own question. 'Who else? I, Zeus, supreme deity and head of this large family, have thought of the solution.'

All of those sublime eyebrows shot up, and the hopeful looks that followed made me tingle with delight. I *am* fond of a little attention now and then.

'Well?' Athena cried, apparently unable to bear the tension a moment longer. 'Tell us, Father!'

I let the silence grow for a second (owning the moment) and then, finally, spoke the five words that would determine our future.

'We are leaving this place.'

Nobody reacted – it was like they'd all been struck by lightning.

'Leaving,' I repeated.

Still no reaction.

'We are leaving here for ever,' I clarified. 'We're gonna bugger off away from this mountain and head for the heights.'

The hall filled with the mumbling of gods, but before the whispering and murmuring could build to yet another raucous dispute, I silenced them all with a mighty gesture. 'We're going to a place where we are needed,' I said. 'Project Earth is officially concluded. On to our next task!'

For a second I thought they hadn't understood me, that I wouldn't be able to prise them away, but then cheers erupted. Dionysus conjured up a fresh load of Coke, musical instruments emerged and everyone started dancing and toasting each other.

'We did it!'

'Yes!'

'Project Earth is completed!'

'Fantastic!'

I sipped my Coke and enjoyed their exuberance. Tomorrow, tomorrow we would leave. And while the celebrations were in full swing, I slipped away unnoticed. It was high time for me to pack my bags.

Or should I just, just once… very briefly… for the very, very last time… go down from the mountain… to spend one more night… yes, just one… among the people below?

Translated from the Dutch by David Colmer

Illustrations by Mårdøn Smet

The Blue Well

Ana Pessoa

I lost my yellow hat at the end of summer, at the end of the mountain.

Mum asked: *How did you lose it?*

I said: *I don't know.*

If I knew, I wouldn't have lost it. I think.

We had gone to the Blue Well. My parents, my brother and I.

None of us knew what the Blue Well was, but Dad had heard that it was a natural pool in the mountains.

I protested: *There's a pool at the camping ground!*

Dad said: *But we've already been to that one.*

I shrugged.

My brother said to me: *Where's your spirit of adventure?*

I said: *I don't know.*

My spirit of adventure had vanished.

Lately I'd only felt like riding in the back seat, watching the world slip past. The houses along the side of the road, the people, the cows. Bends this way, bends that way. The car hugging the mountainside. My eyes at the window. Seatbelt on tight.

Every now and then the mountain would appear in its entirety, and I'd feel uneasy. The valley stretching out to the horizon, like a spell. The mountain so big and us so small.

Sometimes I feel this uneasiness. In churches. At the end of parties. On Sunday nights.

I don't know why. I can't get to sleep. Mum lies down with me and reads me a story or part of a story. Only then do I fall asleep.

Mum reads a lot. Right now she's reading a book called *A Death in the Family*. I don't like that Mum's reading a book called *A Death in the Family*. I'm never going to read that book.

Never never never.

Grandma says I'm a stubborn girl and when I get something in my head, there's no changing my mind.

And it's true. There's no changing my mind.

Dad said: *We're here.*

But we weren't anywhere. I got out of the car and saw the end of the road, the end of the mountain.

My brother said: *This is the end of the world.*

And it was.

I once read a book about the end of the world, but in the last chapter the world didn't end. In the end, the monsters ran away.

When I was five, I thought people were monsters disguised as people, including my parents. As soon as they turned around, they became foxes that weren't exactly foxes.

I believe in monsters. And extraterrestrials.

In front of us was a trail, straight all the way.

Mum said: *Put your hat on.*

I said: *In a minute.*

Mum said: *Put it on now.*

I put on the helmet, which wasn't a helmet. It was my wide-brim yellow hat. It had a long chin strap and little holes at the sides.

Dad looked at me, at the hat on my head, at the top of the hill. He said: *My explorer.*

I laughed, because I'm not an explorer. I'm the opposite. I don't like climbing trees any more, or poking my fingers in the dirt. I don't know why.

Last week I wrote a poem about my hat. It started like this: *My hat was taken by the wind.*

But it wasn't the wind that took my hat.

What was it?

I don't know.

There was no wind in the mountains. Not even a breeze. The sun grinned enthusiastically in the middle of the sky.

I've just realized that *grinned* rhymes with *wind*. I didn't remember that when I was writing the poem.

I like drawing. It's my favourite subject at school.

The day we went to the Blue Well, I drew a dragonfly that didn't look anything like a dragonfly. It looked like a helicopter. Dad tried to help me, but his dragonfly wasn't that good either.

Dad laughs more when he goes walking in the mountains. He's more relaxed, more rustic. Mum says Dad has a little shepherd inside him.

It's possible.

I know my parents have sex, but I've never seen them do it, nor have I ever heard them.

I've never kissed a boy. When I was four, I kissed a girl. She was my best friend. Her name was Francisca. I haven't seen her in ages and I'll probably never see her again. I've lost her for ever.

How did you lose her?

I don't know.

Someone wrote ÉRICA in the bathroom at the camping ground. Just that: the name in capital letters. Whenever I go to the bathroom, I look at that name: ÉRICA. I've never met a girl named ÉRICA. It isn't a common name. I imagine an uncommon girl. Athletic, fast, a winner.

I'd like to be called ÉRICA. Just to see what it's like.

My PE teacher said I lose on purpose. He said I have the legs of a gazelle but I don't run. I never go after the ball.

I think he's right. I'm not competitive. I don't like playing football.

I like to watch the world from a distance. From the back seat.

My brother isn't like me. He doesn't stop for one second. The day we went to the Blue Well, he was always leaving the trail.

Mum said: *Don't go that way*. But he did. My brother in the middle of the rocks, backpack jiggling.

Dad said: *Don't run*. But he did. And he'd shout from down below: *There're goat turds down here*.

Mum would shout: *Don't shout*. But my brother would shout anyway.

At the top of the hill he let out a howl like an animal. It gave me a fright.

My brother said to me: *You're such a scaredy-cat*. And it's true.

The mountain there in the background, lying on its bed of rock. The deep calm of the trees. So focused on living. On solitude. On photosynthesis.

Dad said: *Let's take a photo*.

He rested the camera on a rock and set the timer. Ten seconds.

My parents, my brother and I. On top of the hill, on top of the world. Frozen in time. Smiling for eternity.

The mountain doesn't fit in a photograph. The mountain doesn't fit anywhere. It stretches off into the distance to the end of space, to the end of time.

I felt the distance, I felt time and space, and I don't know if it made me happy or sad. It's strange. I never understand what I feel and sometimes I don't think anyone understands me.

Matilde told me she didn't want to be my friend any more. We were in the bathroom. I asked: *Why?* She said I didn't know how to talk about feelings. I didn't answer. I just stood there. Speechless, unfeeling. I locked myself in a toilet stall to cry. There was no toilet paper. I wiped away my tears and runny nose with my hands.

Mum said: *You're really quiet*. And I was, it's true. I didn't have anything to say, nor did I want anyone to talk to me. I didn't want to be hugged. I didn't want anything at all. I just wanted to exist. Like a piece of mountain. A piece of everything. A piece of nothing. Learn silence. Fly over the landscape.

One day I'd like to be an eagle. Just to be able to see the mountain from above and have a nest at the top.

I believe in reincarnation.

On our way to the Blue Well we passed a little swamp where there were lots of frogs. I croaked with happiness and felt like taking them with me. I also felt like kissing them on the lips. Maybe one would turn into a prince or some other kind of nobleman. Or a normal person. A cook, a computer technician, an ear-nose-and-throat doctor.

I fall in love easily.

On the day of the Blue Well, I fell in love with a shepherd. We were on top of the hill, on top of the world.

Dad said: *Good morning.*

The shepherd said: *Good morning.*

And I began to imagine a life with the shepherd. Our house at the top of the hill, he with his crook in hand, and I with a scarf on my head. We'd be like the mountain. Hard, eternal, unflinching. And we'd never talk about feelings. We'd have hearts of stone.

At one point, we passed a strange tree. It clung to the ground with the tips of its toes and its face was a bit panicky. It looked off-balance. In the middle of the trunk was a dark hole big enough for a person.

My brother said: *What's that?* And he stuck his head in the hole. Mum said: *Be careful.*

My brother said: *I can't see anything.*

My brother and I stood in front of the black hole. My brother was much taller than me, much more alive.

A shiver ran down my spine. I felt uneasy.

I imagined a witch inside the tree. A mirror. An extraterrestrial. A portal to paradise. Or to some other world. The descent to hell.

I'm the only girl in the family. I have ten boy cousins and a brother. Once we had a parakeet and even he was male. I'd like to have a sister or a girl cousin. Just to see what it's like. Perhaps I'd even tell them my wild ideas about the strange tree.

I don't know.

The huge, blazing sun, devouring thought.

Dad said: *When we get there, let's dive in.*

I said: *No way.*

I never dive in. I always jump in, feet first. Or all curled up to do a cannonball.

My brother found two long sticks in the middle of the rocks.

He said: *Want a staff?*

I said: *Yes.*

A long, slightly crooked stick, from my waist to the ground.

I took the staff and felt a new equilibrium. A certain mastery over worldly things.

Dad said: *My explorer.* And I laughed.

Mum said: *There are some horses.*

Where?

Over there.

We watched them from a distance. One of the horses shook its head and looked at me. The strength of a horse in my eyes. I imagined the horse galloping down the mountainside. The wild horse and I. Our fury at a gallop.

To the end of the world, to the end of time.

Suddenly, I tripped.

Mum said: *Watch where you're going.*

I've never ridden a horse.

I've never dived in.

I've never been to a funeral.

A boy from school was run over by a car, but I didn't go to the funeral because I wasn't in his class.

I'd like to have a dead friend. Just to see what it's like.

My brother said: *We must be near the river now.*

And we were.

First there was a wooden bridge and right after it a stream whispering secrets. My blood rushing through my veins, the stream rushing over the rocks.

We plunged our hands into the cold water and our hats too.

We filled our hats with water and put them back on our heads.

Water cascading down our faces. Down our hair, our T-shirts. It was diving the wrong way up.

Dad said: *We must be just about there.*

Turns out we weren't.

It was uphill all the way. My legs were tired. One boulder, another boulder. By a certain point, no one was saying a thing. It was the concentration of the effort, the silence of the exertion. My staff went ahead of me and I followed it, eyes to the ground. We climbed higher and higher.

The sun closer and closer, ablaze. Scorching our moods, our insides.

My brother said: *Is it much further?*

Dad said: *No.*

But we never got there. We were at the end of the mountain, at the end of summer.

I opened my canteen and drank water.

Mum said: *Don't drink all the water.*

Which made me even more thirsty.

Mum said: *You'll want some later and you won't have any.*

I wanted strength, but I didn't have any.

Maybe the Blue Well didn't even exist. Maybe it was a dry basin, a hole in the rocks.

I've never been in a desert, but it can't be very different. The sun and my thirst, the last of my strength.

Then, suddenly, around a bend, behind the hill. A mirage. An oasis. There it was.

The Blue Well.

A hole in the rocks. Full of water and hope. Completely alone.

The sun playing on the water, admiring itself in the mirror. The clouds in duplicate. The entire sky in the Blue Well.

I felt time and space. I felt my existence at a gallop. An unbridled impulse.

This time it was me who let out a howl. On top of the rock, on top of the world.

Me whinnying at life, disturbing the landscape.

My brother laughed, my parents too.

I looked at the mountain, beautiful and enormous. Sitting on its throne of stone, watching the initial plunge.

I was first. I jumped from the highest rock, to do a cannonball.

My existence in free-fall. My existence plummeting into the water that had run off the mountain.

The cold water against my body. Purifying my soul. Refreshing my thoughts.

My whole life. Pure. Wild. Real.

And I felt that I, too, was a piece of water. A piece of mountain, a piece of everything.

I was the silence. The unease. The solitude.

A horse. A frog. An eagle.

My hat. My staff. My childhood.

I was the deep calm. The sun. The mountain.

The distance.

The Blue Well.

Translated from the Portuguese by Alison Entrekin

Illustrations by Helen Stephens

Nearly Home

B.R. Collins

Of course we rushed down there as soon as we could. The only thing I could think about was to get to her and hold her in my arms and tell her it would all be all right. At times like that it's unbearable for a mother to know that her child is suffering miles away. It's easy when they're small: you can wipe their tears and stick a plaster on their scraped knee, but as soon as they're a bit older you can feel so helpless. To be honest, I don't think anyone who isn't a parent can really understand. I'll never forget the shock and desolation of that moment: standing there in the quiet hall with the phone in my hand and the sun streaming through the stained-glass window in the front door, while a quiet voice murmured things about an ambulance, A&E, an emergency scan... It's irrational, I know, but I felt as though *I'd* let *her* down. And the woman from the summer school was quite insensitive – not that she said anything I could have written down and complained about, but her tone of voice was entirely unsympathetic. If I'd had to break that sort of news, I would have made sure I was tactful and considerate, not simply matter-of-fact; you'd think they'd get some sort of training.

I don't know, maybe I'm being a little uncharitable. I wasn't thinking straight, I know that. When she'd rung off I collapsed onto the bottom stair and took a few moments to compose myself before going into George's study and telling him what had happened. He took it in his usual stoical fashion, with only a blink when I said 'pregnant' and another one when I said 'miscarriage'; he's a good man, but he doesn't really *feel* things, if you know what I mean. He'd been in the middle of one of his science projects, and he just turned his fountain pen over and over in his hands while I tried to remember all the details. At last he said, 'Poor sausage,' but just as I reached out to take his hand, he added, 'Well, we'd better jump straight in the car,' and I realized he hadn't meant me.

Naturally I would have loved to throw everything aside and race there like a mad thing, but someone has to be practical and I had an appointment I couldn't rearrange, so in the end it was past midday by the time we set off – and by then the traffic was absolutely awful. It was like a nightmare, sitting on the M25, while all I could think about was Polly in A&E, Polly calling out for her mum, Polly white and ill with her hair sticking to her face… I kept remembering how she'd looked when she had meningitis when she was six, and how I couldn't stop squeezing her hand; the nurse had to peel my fingers away because she was afraid I'd leave a bruise. Love like that is so strong it hurts, it makes you feel physically sick.

Anyway, thank goodness George had dropped Polly off at the beginning of the week instead of letting her take the train, because in the state I was in I would never have been able to find the place on my own. It all passed by me in a blur – wrought-iron gates and a winding gravel drive, a green vista across the grounds with the cathedral in the distance, and then we came round the final curve and there was the house. It was lovely, actually, all grey-gold stone, with a pillared portico, although there was a modern wing which they'd cunningly cropped out of the photograph on the website. It's funny how you notice things, even when you're crazy with worry. I got out of the car and took it all in while I waited for George – he seemed to take ages, fiddling with the keys – and I was glad that at least Poll had had a few days in this beautiful place, before everything went so wrong.

The lady at reception showed us into an elegant green-and-grey drawing room that looked out onto a formal garden. 'Polly's in here,' she said. 'She's been waiting since half-past nine.'

'Poll, darling…' I can't tell you how good it felt to put my arms round her. But when at last I stepped back and saw her face, I was surprised and pleased at how normal she looked. She was wearing make-up, which normally I don't like, but obviously it meant she wasn't feeling too upset or ill. 'Oh, sweetheart, I'm so sorry.'

'I'm fine, Mum.' Poll pushed past me and hugged George, which I was glad to see. (I do often wonder whether she thinks George doesn't love her as much as I do.) 'Hello, Dad.'

'Hello, love. How are things?'

'OK.'

'Let's get you home, darling,' I said. 'There's nothing to worry about. We're here now.'

She nodded and reached for her bag, but George swung it over his shoulder before she got her hand on the strap. She rolled her eyes – she was clearly perfectly capable of carrying it herself – but he set his face in mock-mulish defiance and in the end she laughed and let him take it. When we got back to the car I squeezed his hand for that, because he may not be very good at expressing emotional support but at least he tries.

We drove in silence for a while. I didn't want to pressure her into talking, but I knew how hard it must have been for her and I wanted her to know that she could tell us anything. In the end I cleared my throat and said, 'Well, darling, how are you feeling?'

'Fine.'

'It sounds like it must have been quite dramatic.'

She didn't answer. I contorted myself to catch her eye in the rear-view mirror, but she was staring out of the window. Really, you would never have known that anything had happened to her; she had that blank, hostile, teenagery expression on her face that makes you feel utterly useless. I took a deep breath and said, 'You know, darling, I had a miscarriage, before you were born.'

'Yes, I know.'

'They're a very common thing. And – well – it's the best outcome, really, isn't it? You must have been so worried when you discovered you were pregnant.' I bit my lip. I wasn't angry with her, of course, but it's terribly difficult to find out, even afterwards, that your fifteen-year-old daughter has been expecting a baby... George didn't seem to have taken it in at all.

Silence. I knitted my fingers together until the rings dug painfully into my knuckles. 'You know we love you, sweetheart. We'll see you through this. Whatever I can do, to make you feel better...'

I wanted her to lean forward and stroke my shoulder with one finger, the way she would have done when she was small. But her only response was a quirk of the mouth that wasn't even a smile and a muttered 'Thanks, Mum'.

I leant back, trying to swallow the ache in my throat. I know you can't expect children to understand how hard it is to be a parent – you run up against it again and again – but it breaks your heart. 'Whatever we can do,' I said again, but this time it was more for myself, a kind of private vow. That's real love, isn't it? When it doesn't matter whether the other person is grateful… George slipped me a glance and patted my knee, and I felt a flicker of comfort.

After that, we drove in silence. I was dreading George asking inappropriate questions, like who was the father, or when was she intending to tell us, or indeed what the hell was she thinking? But he managed to restrain himself, and after a while I heard the scratch of Poll's headphones. Every so often I sneaked another look at her. She was a little pale, as you'd expect from the blood loss, but I could see that the whole thing had hardly touched her: she's inherited George's temperament, which I'm grateful for, and in any case she's still enough of a child not to feel anything very deeply. It was a wonderful relief to know that she wasn't suffering the way I had, after my miscarriage – but then that was very different. Polly didn't want a child, she's a fifteen-year-old with a wonderful musical career ahead of her.

At last we came off the motorway and down the A21, and then we turned down the London Road and we were nearly home.

We passed the post office, and I sat up and craned my neck to look: for once it didn't have a queue snaking out onto the pavement outside. 'Oh good,' I said, grabbing George's arm, 'pull in here.' It was a little thing, but in the rush that morning I'd forgotten to post Aunt Harriet's card, and it had to go to the United States, and so it was a godsend to have remembered just as we drove past. 'Wait here – I won't be a moment…'

'What? I thought we were going home,' Polly said.

'Aunt Harriet's card, darling. It's her ninetieth. I've got it in my bag. It won't take a minute.' Poll's never been one for thinking about other people, but I kept my voice kind.

'Can't you do it another time? Dad, please can we just go home?'

He twisted round to look at her. 'What's the matter, love?'

'I don't want to stop here. Can we park somewhere else?'

I was already halfway out of the car – looking undignified, I dare say – but George actually put his indicator on as if he was about to drive away. 'George! Honestly, Poll…' She'd pushed herself into the corner of the seat and was shielding her face with her hand, so that I wondered if she'd seen someone she knew; but when I looked, there was nothing but the window of Mothercare, full of car seats and toys and faceless child mannequins. It was all rather horrid colours, nothing that you would actually want to dress a child in. 'Oh, darling, don't be so silly,' I said. 'It's only Mothercare.'

'I don't want to look at it right now, Mum. Please.'

'Oh…' I hesitated. But it's always murder trying to find somewhere to stop on the High Street, and I'd been lucky to spot somewhere to pull in; and my shoes had given me a blister on my heel, and if we parked farther away I'd end up being in pain for days. And after all it was only because of her that I'd forgotten to post the card after my hair appointment that morning. 'You don't really mind, sweetie,' I said. 'It's only a nasty old shop window – it won't hurt you. I won't be long. Just close your eyes or something.'

'Mum, for God's sake—'

'Give me two minutes,' I said, and shut the door.

It took a little longer than that, to be fair, but it was definitely quicker than it would have been for me to come all the way back after we'd dropped Polly at home. When at last it was done I scampered out of the door, making a little performance of hurrying towards them, to lighten the mood a bit. George looked up and smiled – although he had that gormless look he always gets when he's left alone with Poll, poor darling – and leant over to push the door open for me. I slid into my seat and said, as I put on my seatbelt, 'There, sweetheart. It's all over now. You see, that wasn't too, *too* awful, was it?'

She got out of the car and slammed the door. It was so sudden I hardly took it in: one moment she was glaring at me from the back seat, the next she was running off down the pavement, nearly cannoning into a young mother with a pushchair. I caught my breath. George was staring after her, his hand poised on the ignition button as if he didn't know what to do.

'My goodness,' I said, 'how silly. What a fuss about nothing.'

George didn't answer. I could have slapped him for the expression on his face; but then he's a man, and they don't feel things the way we do.

We watched Polly run up the street, her flip-flops flapping, one awkward hand holding her hair out of her face. And for a second I saw the child she'd been five years ago – ungainly, impulsive, delightful, with a messy plait that swung like a bell rope and a temper that turned from sun to storm in no time at all. She hadn't really changed: she was still that Poll, deep down – *my* Poll. In a strange, perverse way I was grateful that she'd been so childish: it reminded me how much of a blessing it was, that this had all blown over so cleanly. It would be years before she was ready even to think of being a mother, if she ever really was.

I didn't say it aloud, though, because I love her, and I didn't want to be unkind.

Illustrations by Kitty Crowther

Mine

Sarah Crossan

I know it's well weird
but I can't stop myself
        climbing into the white cot,
lying, crunched up
on the quilt Karen made herself
and staring
at the ceiling fan.
Dad had it fitted last week
when
it got so hot Karen
decided the weather
could kill a new-born.

'We have to have a fan, Danny.
We just *have* to,' she said,
and Dad
Made It Happen
cos that's his mission now —

to be a Good Dad,
best ever, in fact.

Sometimes though,
it's like he's forgotten he's still got me,
and I'm only twelve
which leaves tons of time
to turn into a total
Nightmare.

      I mean,
if he isn't very vigilant
I might transform into a
dead beat, dropout delinquent
spraying graffiti on underpasses
with my drug-addict mates.

It's possible.

He should be careful.

God,
I bet there wasn't all *this* bother when I was born –
matching curtains, carpet, a special chair for the nursery.
Even the name Karen's given the baby's room,
      The Nursery,
is over the top.
Why can't it be called
      The Baby's Room
in the same way mine's called
      Stacey's Room.

Maybe I should come up with a new name
for where I sleep,
call it

The Academy,
which sounds sort of special –
like some NASA training space.

Dad's painted the wall of
The Nursery
lime green
with orangey edges
cos
they don't know yet whether
they're landing me with a brother or a sister.

They could find out,
        of course,
ask the nurse doing the scan
whether or not she can see a wormy willy
between the legs of the baby.
They want it to be
'a surprise'
though,
like having a baby won't be a big
enough
shock,
like maybe the midwife
will hand over an adorable diplodocus
instead of a child.

Now that *would* be a surprise.
Even I'd be on board
waiting to hear that kind of news.

And that's what I'm lying here waiting for.
News from the hospital.

A brother or a sister?

So what.
It'll still scream and puke
my life to pieces.

Anyway
it is cosy in this cot.
Sort of a tight squeeze
but
I actually like the bars.
Doesn't feel like a prison,
more a cocoon,
somewhere super safe,
and I think Nan's fallen asleep in front of the TV
so I can lie here as long as I want.

Well, until they come home.

With the baby.

The baby,
a whole new person
who'll own this whole cot,

Nursery,
probably all Karen's time
and most of Dad's.

Thing is,
Dad's forty-five
and already got grey hair,
way too old for another kid.

It's embarrassing
and no one can see it
except me.
Everyone else on the planet is all,
That's wonderful news!
and
Oh, a baby, how nice!
and
Congratulations!

No one says,
Aren't you a bit long in the tooth, Danny,
or
Could you even catch a running toddler?
or
What the hell have you done?

My mate Marissa
says I'm just jealous
cos in a dark part of my heart
I think the
baby will be better than me,
and loved harder than me,
and I'll end up on the rubbish heap
for kids
no one wants.

She didn't say it exactly
like that
but I got her meaning.

Thing is,
I reckon she's wrong.

I'm not jealous.

It's jealousy to want someone's bike
or brains
or boyfriend.

I don't want anything Baby's got,
apart from this cot maybe,
and the cosy quilt.

I just wish it could belong to another couple
so my house
doesn't get turned
        upside down
        inside out
while everyone calculates how to
cope with a tadpoley person.

I curl my arm around the fluffy
cuddly
bunny
Nan bought for Baby.

It tickles my nose
and I smile.

Gosh,
it really is snuggly in here.

I might ask Dad for
a king-sized cot of my
own,
a cool room with
        a ceiling fan
and limey-green walls.
I put my thumb in my mouth and suck on it.
That's nice too.
A dummy might be even nicer.

Thing is,
usually I have to sneak in here
when Mum and Dad
are asleep,
tiptoe passed their bedroom
and hope they won't wake
while I'm daydreaming of nothing,
careful not to doze,
trying to imagine being in the skin
of a teeny, tiny thing,
kicking legs that can't walk,
just toddle,
and a mouth that waffles
ga-ga-ga.

I can't remember what sort of room I had,
whether or not my mum ever handmade a quilt for *me*.
The photos
Dad's got of her
give the impression she wasn't that sort of mother –
not a quilter, a baker, a knitted-scarves maker.

I could ask Dad what it was like
        back then.

But I haven't.

He's too excited
and talking about Mum would probably
depress him.

Depresses me.

But.

Anyway.

'Stacey, love!' Nan calls from downstairs.
'What you doing?'

I wish I could stay silent,
pretend to be asleep.
But then she'd come upstairs,
see me
and blab to Dad and Karen.
Then
when I'm nineteen,
it would be
One of Those Stories
everyone knows

and finds hilarious –
the time I got caught in the cot
pretending to be a baby.

'I'm reading, Nan!' I shout.

'You're what?'

'Reading!'

'Oh, for goodness' sake, Stace,
come down here and watch
Strictly with me
will you?
I'm making tea and toast.'

'Ugh!'

'What?'

'I said one minute.'
I climb out of the cot.
I don't want to.

The bunny looks up at me with
blue icy eyes.
'What do *you* want?' I ask.
It stares.
The bunny.
The eyes unbreakable.
What if Baby chews on them though?
Wouldn't it choke?

I pull the bunny through the bars
and stuff it under my T-shirt,
trudge downstairs
where Nan is standing in front of the open fridge
sniffing at a carton of milk.

She turns.
'Is this sour?
I can't tell.'

'What's the date on it?'

'Oh, I don't trust supermarkets
with their best-befores.
No, no, no.'

I go to her and sniff the milk.
'Smells all right to me,' I say.

It's raining.
The sheets on the line are dripping wet.
Karen will complain.
She'll say Nan is useless
and we should've had
her mum come to take care of me
and lend a hand.

'I'm going to Dad's shed,' I say.

'You are not.
The toast will get cold.'

'So?
I like when it's cold and the butter doesn't melt.'
I slip my feet into a pair of Karen's wellies.

'You're the strangest girl,' Nan says,
and kisses my forehead.

I push open the back door and run to the shed,
rain pelting me,
which is nice
when it's hot like this.

Dad's shed is a mess.
Paint pots and bits of wood everywhere,
two broken radios,
a pile of newspapers with the crosswords only half-finished.

And on the back wall, plastic boxes –
screws and nails and pins.
I reach under my T-shirt and take out the bunny,
put her on Dad's workbench.

She looks alarmed.

And she should.

I go to a plastic box,
find nails as long as crayons,
bring them back to the bench
and with the tip of one,

unpick the bunny's tummy stitches.
It's an intricate operation
but my hands are steady.
And when there's just enough space,
I push a nail through it,
inject the bunny with metal,
outstare her when she protests.
'What?' I ask.
The bunny is sweet but she can't speak.
She has no words to warn anyone.
Ga-ga-ga.

I push the other nail through,
pinch the seams together again
so no one will see the hole.
'There,' I say. 'Lovely.'

Back in the house Nan is jiving in the living room,
copying the contestants on TV.
She looks at me.
'You're soaked.'

'I'm OK.'

The tea and toast is on the coffee table,
precariously perched by the edge
and ready to get tipped
when Nan twirls
and ruin Karen's cream carpet.

I slurp from the mug.
Nan's mobile jangles
and Dad's name pops up – *DANNY.*
'Get that,' Nan says,
twirling.

I slide my thumb across the screen.
'Hey Dad,' I say.

'Stacey!' His voice is a song.

'Yeah?'

'Oh, Stacey.'

'What?' I ask.

'It's the baby,' he says.

'What?'

'It's been born.'

'Huh?'
I'm confused.
I want him to know I'm very confused.

'Yes. I know,' he says.
I think he might be crying.
'It took less than two hours.
Karen's knackered but she's delighted.'

'A baby?' I ask.

'Huh?' he says.

'You have a new baby?'

'Stacey?' he says.

Nan stops spinning.

Turns off the TV.
'A baby? Well?'

'Nan says *well*,' I tell him.

'She what?'

'She says well.'

'Stacey. You have a sister,' he says.
'Her name's Wendy.
You have a little sister called Wendy
and I have to admit
she's way uglier
than you
but she's lovely.
And we are in love with her.'

'Huh?'

'Stacey?'

'Dad?'

'Yeah?'

'I lost the bunny,' I say.
'I mean I have to throw it away.
It got ruined in the rain.'

'The bunny? What bunny?'

'Wendy's bunny,' I say.

'I don't remember the bunny,' he says.

'That's your bunny,' Nan announces.
'I bought that for you.
Did Karen think it belonged to the baby?'

'Would you like to come to the
hospital
and meet your sister?' Dad asks.

The bunny is back in the shed.
I won't put it into the cot like I planned.
I don't think I will.
Not today anyway.
No.

'Stacey?' Dad says.
'What do you think?'

'The bunny's mine,' I say.

'Huh?'

'The bunny's mine,' I repeat.

Illustrations by Anke Kuhl

#Parisjetaime

Sanne Munk Jensen

Joachim is rummaging through his bag for an apple. He hasn't said anything and I didn't see him put one in his bag at the hotel, but I know that's what he is doing. He always keeps an apple in his bag. Always red and always covered in bruises, because it has been knocking about between water bottle, book and camera for hours. And then at some point, when a natural pause arises, like now, when according to the departure board it is nine minutes until our Metro arrives, he rifles through his bag and pulls it out.

'Would you like a bite?' he asks. Not now, in a moment. I know he will. And no, I would not like a bite. I have never said yes, but he asks every time.

At one time I might have thought it was sweet. Polite. At one time I might even have enjoyed watching him eat the apples. I don't remember.

He rubs the apple against his trousers.

'Would you like a bite?'

The hotel room had a view of the Seine, it had a tall sofa with polished wood and pink-and-gold satin upholstery. Its legs curved like lazy S's, pencil-thin, making it look like Pumbaa from *The Lion King*. It was the first thing I thought of when I saw it, but I did not mention it.

I fell back onto the large double bed. It was not as soft as it looked. Quite the opposite, in fact. I did not mention that either. I just lay completely still with my hands under my head observing Joachim, who had placed his suitcase on a stool and was putting his clothes in the cupboard. He had removed his shirt and was standing in his underwear. He had nice arms. He had always had nice arms. Judging by his arms and upper body alone, you could definitely not tell that he was almost nine years older than me.

I pulled my blouse over my head and removed it. Turned onto my side with my head resting on my upper arm. Patted the bed.

'Why don't you come lie down for a bit?'

Joachim looked at his watch. Exhaled heavily.

'There's no time for that,' he said. 'I booked a table for seven o'clock, and I need to grab a shower first.' He raised one arm and took a whiff. 'I'm a bit sweaty.'

He folded his trousers and boxers over one arm and grabbed a hanger with a shirt and went into the bathroom. Turned on the shower.

Hanging above the stool was an oil painting: it looked like something I had to discuss for my final oral exam in Danish just before summer holidays. It depicted an arrangement of food. Ham, sausage, fruit and a dead bird. A pheasant or something. Its head was hanging down, staring vacantly into the room with a half-open glossy eye and its beak agape, as if it had just been throttled to death. Its small, fat tongue was visible inside its beak, and it made me think of something Sophia had said when she and Adam returned from their trip to the Far East, that bird tongues were a delicacy there. They had not tried them, though they had eaten a hash pizza and had sex for four hours afterwards. Adam had even taken his diving certificate there, but we calculated that, if you added everything up, then our five days in Paris would still end up costing more than their month and a half of backpacking. I don't remember why, but when we discussed it, for some reason I felt like I had won.

At the breakfast buffet there were thousands of things to choose from, and each morning I thought: I wish we could just stay here, drinking juice and tea and eating mini-croissants as people come and go. We could just chit-chat about something personal – I have no idea what it might be, we could just make up things about who all the people were. Where they came from and what they were talking about in their various languages. But there was no time for that. I didn't even ask, but I knew. After coffee, Joachim pulled out his phone and we went over all the things we wanted to fit in. The museums. The squares. The churches. The shops he wanted to check out. He entered the routes into Google Maps. Day one: Montmartre, ten o'clock. Metro to Notre-Dame. Light lunch. Then the Louvre, but the queue was so long that we dropped that, otherwise there wouldn't be time for the shops.

'Sound good to you?' Joachim asked; I nodded and said it was fine, I didn't know anything about paintings anyway.

Joachim bought two shirts and a tie at a shop on the Champs-Élysées. We were in the shop for what felt like a hundred years, and I sat on a small stool while he tried them on. I texted Sophia, but she didn't reply. Posted a picture of our lunch on Instagram. A close-up of a croque-madame, an Orangina and Joachim's hand holding an espresso in a lo-fi filter. #Parisjetaime #Lunch #Love.

'I'd like to buy you a dress, if you fancy,' he said when he emerged from the shop. He was in a good mood. He always was after buying new clothes.

'That one, for example. That's really my style.' He put his arm round my shoulder and nodded at a shop window where there was a mannequin wearing a dress that appeared to be in two parts. The lower half was black and the upper half was white. 'Super elegant, a real classic. You can wear it tomorrow when we go to the opera.'

'That's a Gucci…' I said and looked at him. Smiled. 'It's fucking expensive.'

'Now, now,' he mumbled without removing his gaze from the dress, and I sensed it at once, the smouldering in my throat and the blurred gaze. I tried to slow my breathing, control it. Blinked. I don't know why, but I pictured it again, the dead bird in the painting, and for some reason I thought of my mum: she was a home carer and she could conduct a perfectly normal conversation with Jarl, a man of over ninety who had Tourette's and every other minute asked if he could see her tits.

'No, Jarl, you may not,' she would say, in the same tone as if he had asked her for the time, and then they'd continue chatting, completely undaunted, and soon Jarl would ask her again. Not because he actually wanted to see her tits, but because there was something inside him that meant he could simply not stop asking. As if it was out of his hands.

'Would you like to try it on?' Joachim looked at me. I cleared my throat and took a deep breath. Smiled. Flashed some teeth. Took his hand and squeezed it.

'I would love that.'

Back at the hotel I took a picture of the Gucci shopping bag and posted it on Instagram. #Gucci #Parisjetaime. Almost immediately I had more than twenty likes, and Sophia asked what it was. *Wait and see*, I replied.

The following evening I took a photo of myself in the full-length mirror before we went out for dinner and the opera. Red lipstick, hair up. Found a filter that made the cut of the dress and the contrast between the black and white appear even sharper, and wrote: *On my way to the opera*. #Tristanandisolde #Gucci #Parisjetaime. Notifications poured in while we were in the taxi, a jumble of likes and emojis and comments, and my phone whirred incessantly. About how fantastic I looked. How lucky I was.

We shared a bottle of rosé over dinner and drank champagne in the foyer of the opera. Two glasses. I don't know if that's what did it, the alcohol, if it somehow peeled away a layer of armour, or if it was a sense of the grandiose that struck me like a body blow, but sitting there in the fifth row when the music began, the moment Isolde began to sing, I was so close to tears that I had to clench my fists so tightly that my nails dug into my palms. I sat like that during the entire first act. I didn't understand a word of what they were singing, not even with the English surtitles, but it all felt like a tsunami that repeatedly rushed out and hit me and dragged me along with it.

I looked at Joachim. He was asleep.

In the intermission we had more champagne, and after the final act I wanted to go to a bar, but Joachim said he was tired. After all, we had a long day tomorrow. Departure and all that.

We returned to the hotel, and Joachim zipped down my dress. I knew what was about to happen, and I wanted it. I wanted him to take the dress off. To hell with how much it had cost. Just tear it to shreds and throw me on the bed and take me wildly and fiercely, like never before; and afterwards he would *not* go to the toilet with the duvet wrapped around him and return to hand me some toilet paper and talk about what time he should set the alarm and ask if I wanted to take a shower first. He would just fall asleep on top of me, exhausted and spent.

But he did not do that. He carefully lifted the dress over my head and hung it on a hanger. In the meantime I unhooked my bra.

I lay down on the bed and Joachim crawled on top of me. I grabbed his hair. Kissed him. Moaned. Tried to push his head down between my legs but somehow he managed to duck his head. I squirmed beneath him. Pushed his shoulders away. He looked at me.

'What are you doing?' he whispered.

'Can't you just... just try something.'
I groaned, and his entire body slowly stiff-
ened, almost like his battery had died.

He blew a lock of hair off his forehead.
Said that maybe we should just leave it.
Maybe it was a stupid time. We did have to
get up early. He rolled off of me and lay down
next to me, on his back, his arm resting on
his forehead. I looked at him. Reached over
and turned his face towards me.

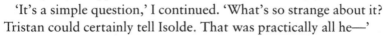

'Do you love me?'

'What kind of thing is that to ask?' he
mumbled, then twisted his neck away so
that my hand slipped off his chin.

'It's a simple question,' I continued. 'What's so strange about it?
Tristan could certainly tell Isolde. That was practically all he—'

'Come on... Would you stop all that nonsense?' he interrupted.

'Nonsense? Is it nonsense? Why can't you just tell it as it is?' My
voice sounded shrill and unfamiliar, kind of like when you plonk
your entire forearm down on the keys of an untuned piano, and I
could sense it again. That feeling. In the throat. In the stomach. It
contracted and throbbed and almost hurt. 'Do you love me? Yes or no?'

He looked at me.

'What do you think?' he said. Loudly. 'Do you think I would have
been with you this long, and... And do you think I brought you to
Paris and to the opera and bought you a Gucci dress if I didn't love
you? Well? Is that what you think?'

'But why can't you just say it?...' I whispered.

'But I do. OK. I love you. Are you happy now?' He ran his hands
through his hair. 'Jesus Christ.'

I didn't reply. Even though I knew the answer perfectly well and could
feel it eating into every single cell in my body. No. I was not happy.

I clenched my fists tightly, tighter than at the opera, but it didn't
help. My entire upper body was twitching.

'You're drunk,' he whispered.

'Like hell I am.'

'Oh. Why are you crying, then?'

'Can't a person cry without being drunk?'

He sighed again.

'Stop carrying on. You're really drunk. And I'm sorry, but this is just a little too childish.'

I didn't reply. Just turned onto my side and pulled the duvet right up over my mouth. Stared at the painting with the food and the dead bird. A fly was resting on one of the apples to the right of the bird's gaping beak. I hadn't noticed it before and I couldn't decide if it was even a part of the painting. It didn't move. Didn't budge, but when my gaze lowered and fell on the dress hanging over the chair, and I looked up at the picture again, it was as though it had moved. Not much. Just a tiny bit. First to the right. Then to the left and closer to the bird. I don't know if it was because I really was drunk or something else, but suddenly I felt I truly understood the painting, and without knowing precisely what I would say, I felt like I could talk about it for hours, for an eternity almost, and it annoyed me that now wasn't the moment I'd got it as the topic for my final oral examination. At least I would have been able to say more than just the title and what it depicted, and I would definitely have got higher than a C.

I heard Joachim's breathing behind me. It grew calmer. Very slowly. Until finally it sounded normal.

He cleared his throat.

'I set the alarm for seven,' he said. 'Do you want to shower first?'

'Mm.'

When he turned onto his side, I considered switching the light on again. Just briefly, to see if it was still there, the fly.

I don't look at him but I know exactly how he is sitting on the yellow plastic seat next to me. Legs crossed. Book in one hand. Apple in the other. I know how the sinews in his neck strain every time he takes a bite; soon he will wipe his mouth with the back of his hand.

A through train thunders past.

I turn my head. Joachim moves the apple towards his mouth, my pulse is pounding. In my neck, throughout my body.

'Do you want to see my tits?' I ask, and he narrows his eyes.

'Sorry, what did you say?' he asks. Lowers the apple and leans towards me.

The last carriage disappears.

'Nothing,' I say. Look up at the board.

'Not the next one but the one after that,' he says. 'The pink one.' I nod.

His teeth slice through the apple like a butter knife through a dry block of florist foam, and it feels like the noise is growing in my head. Louder and louder, until it is drowned out by the next train as it glides into the station. The doors open. A man is sitting inside playing the drums. Bongo drums. He's black. I don't understand why he's playing, because there is no hat or violin case to throw money into. He's just doing it.

My hand closes around the handle of the suitcase. It's surging inside me. Insanely loud and frantic. An entire sea in turmoil. A tsunami. Now or never. That's what I'm thinking.

I brush a fly off my arm. Get up and grab the suitcase.

'What are you doing?' Joachim asks.

'It's not you,' I say. 'Sorry.'

But I don't think he hears me. Not properly.

I walk up to the door and board the train.

'But that's not our train!' Joachim shouts behind me. 'It's the next one! Hey! *That's the wrong train!*'

The train lets out a screech, the doors close and the carriage jolts to life. The man with the bongo drums smiles at me.

I smile back.

'Phew,' I say, even though I know he doesn't understand. 'Just made it.'

Translated from the Danish by Paul Russell Garrett

Illustrations by Yvonne Kuschel

Out There

Victor Dixen

For the first fourteen years of my life, I never even dreamt of what else there might have been, way out there.

'You're a man now, Thibaut,' my father declared solemnly on the morning of my fifteenth birthday, holding out a new rifle. 'Now listen to me: a man's job is to defend the land that has been passed down to him, the land that nourishes him, where his roots are. Just like your ancestors, who over the generations transformed a simple little farmhouse into a mansion, and a small plot of land into a great farming estate. I'll be counting on you to repel the starlings that threaten our harvests, and to rout the brigands who have their eye on our cattle. It will also be your job to levy a suitable tribute on the wild geese that fly over our swamps every year.'

I took the rifle from my father's hands. It was heavy as a new responsibility, a piece of ballast that made me instantly more important.

But my mother gave a little cough, raising her head from the fat ledger where each evening she made a record of the estate accounts; in her light eyes I could see myself still a child, and understood that she had not given her agreement to what was happening.

'Our well-placed scarecrows chase off more starlings than a few gunshots,' she said in her usual gentle voice. 'Well-maintained enclosures can protect the cattle, day and night, far more effectively than a guard who might doze off at any moment. As for the wild geese, hunting season won't begin for several long months yet. Thibaut is still a little young to have his own rifle.'

When she said this, I had the impression that it was my own season to which she was referring, my age as a man that had not yet begun.

'You're quite right, my dear,' agreed my father, to my great dismay, smoothing his greased moustache. 'In the spring, the geese will come back up from *out there*, in the hot countries' – he gestured vaguely with his right hand, indicating the distant lands where the oranges and spices grow – 'and go to make their nests *up there*, in the cold countries.' He sketched a vague movement now with his left hand, towards the likewise unknown regions where the wolves and the reindeer run.

Then he turned towards me:

'The law requires that we wait till the geese come back down with their broods, in the autumn, to hunt them. There's no reason you can't wait, too, Thibaut. Hand me back that rifle: I'll put it away there, in the sideboard, until September.'

I nodded, and went up to bed.

But before dawn had broken the next morning, I tiptoed down, opened the sideboard, took out the rifle and set off towards the swamps.

I remember the warm wood of the rifle butt in the hollow of my neck, and the cold metal of the barrel between my fingers, as I lay there in ambush amid the reeds.

Drapes of mist hung over the low black waters, inhabited by invisible presences just awakening after the winter. Heavy clouds stretched out across the damp March sky, still faltering between night and day. Everything, all around me, was silent. All I could hear was the whistle of my own breathing and the accusing voice of my conscience.

Taking that rifle without permission, you're no better than a thief! it reproached me, to which I replied in my head, *My father gave me this rifle: you can't steal what already belongs to you!*

And going off to hunt out of season, you're no better than a poacher! it spoke again. *I'm in my own home,* I answered it – *you can't be a poacher on your own land!*

As time passed, the heavier the rifle seemed, and the more I felt my muscles weakening, painful from the lack of movement and the cold. I knew I ought to be back before nine o'clock was rung on the village bells, to prepare myself for Sunday mass.

Just as I was about to give up, I heard them: the first geese of spring.

Then I saw them. They split the sky like a vast arrow, in the V-shape they form to cross the world.

I cocked my gun.

And I fired.

Just once, at the point of the arrow, the angle of the V, at the one bird that was opening the way to all the rest.

It spun down to the surface of the swamp, a fine gander with silvery plumage, more impressive than any I had seen before. As I watched its majestic body sink into the waters, my anger dissipated, my frustration melted away. I felt like a real man. I pulled my boots from the mud; I returned to the still-sleepy house; I put the rifle away in the sideboard, deciding not to touch it again before the autumn.

Summer followed on from spring just a few weeks later, as eager to arrive as I was to grow up.

That year, our orchards brought early fruit, as fat as balloons and sugary as candy. Our fields were covered in a sea of green ears of wheat, tender, thick and dense. The calves born to our cows grew faster, fed on more succulent grass. From morning to night I rode across the estate alongside my father, who treated me as his equal now and said over and over: 'Keep your eyes open, son, and learn from what you see, because one day all this will be yours.'

Our sharecroppers and our farmworkers addressed him as *boss*, naturally, but they no longer called me *Young Thibaut* or *Taubi* like they'd done the year before: now I'd become *Monsieur Thibaut*. Each time they uncovered their heads in my presence, I was transported with pride and gratitude. I also felt the weight of a serene duty: to continue to make the farm prosper when it was under my charge, in order to secure these people's future and my own.

It was in late June, as the wheat was starting to turn gold and to produce its grain, that the farmworkers mentioned the presence of wild geese just outside the fields.

'Geese, in this season?' exclaimed my father. 'Impossible! They're all up there' – he gestured – 'somewhere in the north of the world, those places where they say the days never end, and they won't be coming back over our lands till it's time for their migration in the autumn. You must have overdone it on the wine at lunch, lads, and got yourselves confused by some fat starlings!'

But the following morning, the ripest of our fields had been devastated. Mere starlings could never have flattened a whole plot like that. As for the long grey feathers left here and there among the ears of corn, emptied now of their grain, they really were the feathers of wild geese...

'Perhaps they're just a few of the migratory birds who've lost their way; maybe some of them are late?' suggested my mother that evening at dinner.

That night for the first time I thought back to that large silvery gander I had shot down in the spring. I had an odd feeling, a vague guiltiness that I hastened to suppress: sure, I had broken the law, but all I'd done was kill a bird! I ended up falling asleep in the middle of the baking-hot night, a sleep that was inhabited by long sandy steppes battered by cold winds, onto which shone a sun that never set.

The geese were not late, nor had they lost their way. They came back the following day, and the day after that, and in ever-increasing numbers. When they crashed down onto a field at dawn or dusk, the scarecrows and the farmworkers were unable to chase them away.

What had been proclaimed days earlier as the best harvest of the decade was turning into an agricultural disaster before our very eyes.

'Enough!' raged my father one morning in July. 'I've written to the Prefect to ask for special dispensation on the hunting dates. Thibaut, fetch your rifle: we're going to show these creatures that've flown in from some place or other just who are the masters here!'

For the first time in months, I opened the door of the sideboard and laid my hands on the rifle. Despite the summer heat, the touch of the barrel froze my fingers like a sliver of ice.

We pulled on our boots and went down to the swamps, our spaniel Cerberus on our heels.

As we made our way through the suffocating heat, a jabbering, rumbling noise began to swell and grow, making the bulrushes before us and the earth under our soles tremble.

'What kind of accursed...' exclaimed my father as we rounded the bend where the willow stood.

There were not dozens of wild geese, nor even hundreds, but *thousands*.

This part of the swamp was completely covered in a coat of living feathers, the grey of the adults alternating with the beige of the springtime newborns.

Before we were even able to cock our weapons, Cerberus went wild.

He began to howl at the top of his lungs.

A whirlwind of flapping wings rose up around us. I pretended to take aim but, without really knowing why, I deliberately shot into the empty parts of the sky, not touching a single bird.

When night came, I again dreamt of mysterious lands, of interminable rows of sparkling dunes with nothing to interrupt the sightline – no fence, no stables or bell tower. My breathing was choked by so much infinity, and more than once I awoke dripping with sweat, wrapped in my bedclothes, short of breath, my heart beating painfully in my chest.

Our land of plenty was transformed into a land at war, our fields of abundance into battlefields.

The farmworkers may have covered the wheat with nets, but the geese always ended up tearing through them.

From morning to night, my father and I would lie in wait, without a moment's break, for the arrival of the looters; but for each one we felled, a hundred more appeared in the sky, beating down onto a field at the other end of the estate, and ravaging it before our horses could get us there.

Our employees were talking more and more openly about a curse. One of them, Barnabé, ended up leaving us to offer his labour to a farm at the farthest end of the region, where the yield seemed more promising. Madeleine, our cook, started reciting prayers to St Francis of Assisi: she had seen the good monk surrounded by birds on a window in the church, and she was counting on him to intercede and save us. While she waited, she was obliged to cook goose at every meal. The rich, white meat, of which I had once been very fond, now repelled me as though I were being served my own flesh for grazing; I preferred to conceal it discreetly in one corner of my plate. In any case, my parents barely noticed me. My mother was too busy adjusting the production forecasts to take into account the drop in her ledger, while my father served himself brandy after brandy, muttering curses into his beard. The sight of their troubles tormented me, I felt guilty... But how was I to tell them about the strange connection, so irrational, which had been established in my mind between the death of the first gander of spring and the calamity that had been afflicting us since the start of summer?

I hadn't managed to do it, and I didn't need to: the gypsy woman took care of it for me.

She arrived one late August evening by caravan, ten days after the feast of the Assumption, along the main road that led in from the village. She stopped her old mare in the courtyard of the huge farm building, opposite our house. When Madeleine emerged from the kitchen wiping her hands on her apron to ask what she wanted, she replied that she could read the future in the palm of a hand in exchange for a one-sou coin.

I could see Madeleine was tempted, but at that very moment my mother followed her outside:

'We're not interested in those superstitions, but hang on anyway – here you go...' she said, holding out a coin to the gypsy.

Beneath her slightly rigid principles, my mother had always been goodness personified; despite the reversal in our fortunes, there was no question of a wandering soul passing through her house without receiving alms.

'Madeleine, would you bring this good woman a plate of grilled goose?' she added.

While the cook complied, the gypsy began to examine me with eyes whose outlines were lengthened by the make-up she wore. The more she looked at me, the more uncomfortable I felt, as though she could read what was written in the depths of my heart.

'It's because of you, isn't it?' she said at last in a melodious voice that bore signs of some mysterious accent.

'What... what's because of me?' I stammered.

She made a gesture that encompassed the whole estate:

'These devastated fields. These ditches filled with feathers. These paths strewn with bird droppings. All along my way I heard the geese weeping: they are orphans now, ever since the death of their king.'

My father interrupted her before she was able to say any more.

'That's enough,' he announced, putting the food Madeleine had brought into the gypsy's hands. 'You should leave before the sun sets. You can keep the plate.'

Watching the caravan moving slowly away along the dusty road towards the south, I felt my throat tighten, stifled by all the questions I wished I could ask. What was it that the gypsy had been able to read in me? Where had she come from? Where was she headed now? For the first time in my life, I tried to imagine what there was beyond the meadows and the fields of the estate, farther off than the village church... I realized I couldn't do it, and I had only one wish: to escape once more into my dreams.

At night-time, I flew over the ochre deserts and the red mountains and plunged down sharply into the hot seas of turquoise waters, above which the sky stretched out limitlessly...

'It's all my fault. I killed the king of the geese, and now they are taking their revenge. They've stayed all summer, and they'll stay all winter, pecking everything up to the last grain of this harvest and up to the tiniest seedling of next year's. I must find the gypsy to ask her how to put an end to the curse, before it's too late.'

My parents looked at me, dazed.

It was the first day of September, a week after the gypsy had come through, and I had just confessed everything.

'That woman has put a crazy idea into your head!' exclaimed my astonished mother.

'No, Mother,' I replied, taking her in my arms, holding back my tears. 'The gypsy just gave words to an idea that had already been tormenting me for months.'

'You're not some poor vagrant, you're my heir!' My father became enraged, raising his voice to try and hide his emotion. 'Your place isn't out on the roads, it's on the estate!'

'But it's precisely so I can save the estate that I've got to go, Father...'

Then I thought for a moment, my heart heavy, and added: '...and because I've got a voice inside that's calling me, and I cannot resist it. I love you, my parents; you have given me everything and taught me everything. But I must go. I know it. I... I promise I will return.'

I hugged each of them, then mounted my horse and set out on the highway. Almost obliterated fields and rows of dismembered fruit trees unfolded on both sides.

I set my mount to a trot so as not to have to witness the desolate sight of these ancestral lands, plundered because of me.

At the same moment, a beating of wings rung out, mixing with the clash of the metal-shod hooves on the road. Bursting out of the tall grasses right beside me, a goose took flight, its soft black eye plunging deep into me just as the gypsy woman's had, its wing caressing my cheek.

Then another goose flew up.

And another.

The faster I rode, the more of them there were, whole flocks rising out of the copses and the groves, up towards the sky, towards the south, in the direction where my horse's halter and my whole being were being drawn forward.

It was then that I understood.

There was no curse, there never had been!

The geese hadn't stayed in order to punish me!

They had stayed so I could show them their way – me, the one who had deprived them of their guide. For days on end they had waited patiently for me to take up the torch from the large silvery gander, surviving on our fields while they waited; for nights on end their nomad memories had dissolved into my sedentary dreams, changing me for ever.

They'd taken a rooted farmer, and made him migratory.

They had become my people.

I had become their king.

Amid a vast cloud of clacking wings, I squeezed my calves against my horse's flanks and set off on a gallop as fast as the wind, leading my sisters on towards our common destination, way out there.

Translated from the French by Daniel Hahn

Illustrations by Peter Bailey

Lost in Transformation

Cornelia Travnicek

Lou's name was Lou. Lou had no age. Lou had no gender. At half-past three in the morning, Lou wandered sleeplessly through the apartment's rooms yet again. When Lou looked out of the window, Lou was reflected in the sky, apparently among the stars. Lou turned away and the reflection in the glass vanished.

Beneath Lou only a few lights were shining in the planet-spanning megacity, the parks and the wild areas with their expansive plants nestling within it, resembling sharply outlined patches of dark fur. The streetlight ribbons, like a procession of glow-worms, had long since faded at this time of night. Again, Lou looked around the almost empty bedroom. By the door, the gleaming bronze travelling caskets were waiting for the day to come. It was time to go home. Lou would love, love to go home. But there was no looking forward to it. It was neither the brief period of existence as negative matter during the HS leap, nor the feeling of disembodiment at the start and end of it that was worrying Lou, and definitely not the simple flight in an IP ship. No, Lou had been through all that once before, five terrayears ago. Five terrayears – that was how long Lou had been away from family and old friends. Instead of looking forward to a long-awaited reunion, Lou was nervous.

Lou had never had to deal with fear before. Lou's outsized curiosity had always deflected any fear of potentially worrying things. And again this time, it wasn't really anxiety that Lou felt, but rather an enormous uncertainty. And it was not the journey itself that was keeping Lou awake at night. Or at least not the upcoming one, lying almost tangibly ahead of Lou, limited in time and with a defined destination. No, it was the other one, the one that came after it, that had Lou standing by the window with crossed arms, staring out into the never total darkness: Lou's journey of self-discovery.

In only a week, Lou was meant to acquire a fixed gender and thus also an officially recorded age. The purpose of Lou's journey home was the Mit-Gezda, the time at which Lou would become a man or a woman, and after which Lou's people counted their ages as adult members of society. Lou pressed a hand against the window pane. They were neither a woman's fingers nor the back of a man's hand. It was Lou's hand, had always been Lou's hand. Who would this hand belong to in a few days' time? Lou suppressed the desire to walk over to the door and kick the travel caskets, even just to nudge them ever so gently with one foot. Lou now balled the hand that had just been lying on the window pane into a fist. It was childish to want to kick your own luggage. Childish, childish! scolded Lou.

It was not as though Lou was making a journey into the unknown, or at least not in theory. Lou had very precise knowledge of the physical characteristics of both possible basic forms of their species. In the past, children had been given no explanation at all of what was ahead of them. Prudery had resulted in a ban on showing illustrations and animations of naked bodies and body parts. Lou tried to imagine the horror with which the new adults must have noticed the changes in themselves, knowing what had started them off, but remaining entirely in the dark throughout the whole process about where they would end up.

Man and woman: mentally, Lou had always used the general humanoid term for the forms defined as male and female, rather than those from Lou's home planet.

When they had last called, Lou's parents had pretended not to notice Lou's unease over the decision. Lou's parents did the same as most parents: they ignored the things they themselves had gone through and repeated what they had been told at the time: everyone has to choose. Even if that was not quite true. And how should they answer Lou's questions? If Mother advised masculinity, or Father femininity, Lou would have to assume that Lou's parents were dissatisfied with their own form of existence. But if Mother advised femininity, or Father masculinity, Lou would probably be right to assume that their limited range of experience devalued the advice. After all, who could report back from both points of view, weigh up both options entirely objectively? Officially, there was no difference between the two forms. Everyone has to choose. However, there had been less and less freedom to choose over the last couple of centuries, so that really you couldn't call it a decision at all any more. But people carried on doing so. Even though, by now, the decision consisted of comprehensive psychological tests and interviews aimed at finding out, as scientifically as possible, which body shape most closely resembled your own deepest, innermost understanding, as a result of which your own decision was made utterly unconsciously – and its result was handed out to you by somebody else. To avoid certain problems, or so they said.

Sometimes you heard horror stories of the way it used to be. Although most of them were probably untrue. Hopefully untrue, thought Lou. There were some people who claimed to know how to manipulate the test. And there were always others looking out for that kind of possibility: people who disrespected the female existence, for example. Lou's parents said nothing of the kind. Lou's parents never said anything about it, because they considered themselves excellent parents – people who let Lou choose alone, didn't try to influence the decision. Parents who, for this sole reason, had sent Lou to spend the last five years of the nine-terrayear basic education at an elite school here on Cybele.

Lou leant on the window frame. On the horizon, the triumvirate suns were slowly pushing up between the residential-unit towers. It was going to be a hot day. One of those days when people on Cybele preferred to stay at home. The first Y-glider was in the sky outside Lou's building. Next door, someone switched on the hissing air shower.

There were no men or women on Cybele. The Cybele humanoids were sexless and, to some extent, immortal. Their society reproduced through cloning. So the humanoids from Cybele were asexual, and many other races considered this to be the reason why Cybele had produced generations of great scholars, one after another – or the same ones over and over again, however you wanted to look at it. But artists were rare on Cybele, apart from a few musicians, and writing was limited mostly to well-considered essays, in which elegance resonated in every word. Lou had once heard Mother say that Cybele humanoids knew nothing of passion.

In the areas of the planet that did not host extra-planetary visitors, all inhabitants of Cybele went naked for three quarters of the Cybele year. During this season, fashion accessories served only to decorate the body, not to cover it. Lou had heard a good deal about that, but of course Lou had never been to one of those places. When they had to mix with strangers, the Cybele – who

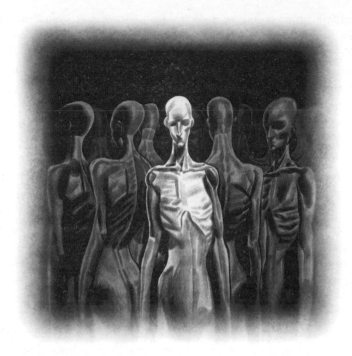

shared the name of their planet – were always clothed to avoid an atmosphere of embarrassing awkwardness. Lou wondered for a moment whether it would be more uncomfortable to be naked among the clothed or clothed among the naked. Probably it came down to numbers: it would be uneasy to be in the minority either way.

Lou had yet to see a Cybele humanoid naked. Truthfully, Lou didn't even want to think about nakedness and bodies any more. Lou hadn't used the shower for the last three days, because every time Lou turned around in the cleansing stream of air it became impossible to avoid thoughts about the future.

The decision to live as a man or a woman would inevitably entail further choices – what career, which residential unit? Lou had heard that they had once tried to fix puberty after tertiary education, because they'd wanted to keep the mind clear of anything that could be a distraction, to keep it childlike, curious, unselfconscious and receptive to learning. But the people in charge had been forced to recognize the need for the brain-restructuring that went along with physical changes at the end of the secondary level. Besides, being too long accustomed to sexlessness often made the transition more difficult and led to more cases of depression. Lou could recite relevant passages from specialist articles on the subject.

Soon someone would come to pick up the luggage, and then... Lou did now walk to the door and kick the caskets, although rather more gently than planned. One of them fell open. Clothes flowed out of it and Lou knew that it was basically pointless to take them home – after all, in a few days Lou would be given a completely new wardrobe of garments for neoadults.

At that moment, Lou's alarm clock went off. Lou hurried over to the bed and put a hand on the alarm sensor to quieten it. As if the alarm would reveal Lou's existence in an act of treachery: Lou's here, Lou's here! Don't forget what day it is!

What if I don't want to? thought Lou again – a question that had kept recurring in the last few Cybele days. What if I just don't want to? There were rumours. There were stories. Stories of religious orders you could join, and of secret societies who spared their members the artificial puberty, were going round among the ageless children at the same stage in their education, many of whom were almost at the point of transition. Some people whispered that you could refuse, that nobody could or would force you, that the only force came from societal convention, the expectations of your family, peer pressure. Officially there were no such cases. But sometimes, sometimes an exception was made for health reasons, Lou had heard, when the hormone cocktail was adjusted, the genetic coding was changed – making it possible to enter adulthood without gender development.

In Lou's memory was a picture of an angel, approaching along a narrow corridor, under soft lighting. The angel was extremely tall, with a bald head and almost black eyes, his slender figure

hidden under the flowing white robes. As Lou looked at the angel in amazement, he returned Lou's gaze, slightly bowing his head and closing his eyelids once, both calming and affirmative, as if he had nodded with his eyes. Lou's mother had taken her child by the hand and pulled Lou on, and Lou remembered having asked: who is that? Mother had smiled and said that it had been a very special person, a spirit being.

Perhaps that spirit had been an asexual, a kind of chosen apparition. Lou sometimes dreamt of being that angel, and each of those dreams had ended with the feeling of the hairless scalp on Lou's left palm.

They say that friendships often fail to survive the transition. Some marry later. Lou was adamant that no friendships should get lost. What if I don't want to? thought Lou again, and more than that: what if it turns out wrong? If nothing fits? If Lou is no longer Lou? Lou lost in transformation.

Lou saw mother's face, talking to Lou from the holoscreen on her comtel: it's really not as bad as all that, Lou.

Now Lou thought there were already steps coming closer to the front door. Tapping on the real-wood-composite floor. That would be the carrier, coming to fetch the travel caskets. The open one was still lying there, like a mussel with its own fabric flesh spilling out of the shell. No pearl. Lou's calf muscles tensed as if warming up for the hundred metres, but Lou didn't know exactly why. Two scenarios were playing out in Lou's head. The porter would come, the door would open, he would stuff the bulging clothes back into the bronze shell, close it and carry both caskets away. Lou would watch it all perfectly calmly and then follow with measured steps. Or maybe the porter would come and, to his astonishment, the door would fly open and Lou would run past him, over the luggage towards an exit. Lou was fast, very fast. So Lou would run to one of the spots of green fur on the planet and vanish into a thicket, and later Lou would struggle on through to one of the regions of Cybele where no one from outside was permitted. There, the Cybele would look at Lou and stare in utter wonder at the strange, clothed child. And Lou would undress, stand naked before the Cybele and say: I belong to you.

Lou heard someone put their hand on the door buzzer, and took a deep breath.

Translated from the German by Rachel Ward

Illustrations by Dave McKean

ABOUT THE AUTHORS

Cathy Clement always wanted to be a writer; her idol was Astrid Lindgren and still is. She was fifteen years old when she wrote *Aleng*, which won the prize for Best Book of the Year in Luxembourg in 1996. With *Aleng* (a kind of diary) she wanted to tell kids facing problems not to give up, not to be ashamed of what they had to go through. Now a nurse with two kids, she has written six novels (five in Luxembourgish and one in German) and a play so far. She is currently working on a new, very personal book called *Not Alone*, while also teaching a vocational course on pastoral care.

B.R. Collins, the daughter of a successful author, has written stories and poems for as long as she can remember. She won the Young National Poetry Competition twice before going on to study English at King's College, Cambridge. Then she trained as an actor at LAMDA, and realized that writing was the perfect way to keep herself sane while she tried to find work. Her first book, *The Traitor Game*, won the Branford Boase Award. Since then she has published six other YA novels with Bloomsbury and been shortlisted for the Stonewall Awards and the Coventry Inspiration Award, as well as being longlisted for the UKLA Award and nominated for the Carnegie Medal several times. She has also had two plays produced.

Sarah Crossan grew up in Ireland and England. She graduated from Warwick University with a degree in Philosophy and Literature, and went on to train as an English and Drama teacher at Cambridge University. She is the author of five novels. In 2010 she was the recipient of an Edward Albee Fellowship and spent the summer in Montauk, New York, working to complete *The Weight of Water*, which was later shortlisted for the Carnegie Medal and won the Eilís Dillon and UKLA book awards. Her novel *Apple and Rain* was also shortlisted for the Carnegie Medal and the FCBG award. Her latest novel, *One*, won the Carnegie Medal 2016, the YA Prize 2016 and the Children's Books Ireland 2016 Book of the Year Award.

Stefanie de Velasco, born in 1978, grew up as a child of Spanish immigrants in the German Rhine Valley. She studied European Ethnology and Political Science and started her writing career as a ghostwriter. Her debut novel *Tigermilch* (*Tiger Milk*), published in 2013, was widely praised and long-listed for the 2015 *Independent* Foreign Fiction Prize. It was made into a film in 2016.

Victor Dixen, the son of a Danish father and a French mother, travelled around Europe with his parents as a kid; as an adult he has kept his taste for travels and storytelling. He has lived in Dublin, Singapore and Denver, drawing inspiration from these different places. He currently divides his time between New York City and Paris. He won the Grand Prix de l'Imaginaire Jeunesse twice, in 2010 for *The Strange Case of Jack Spark* and in 2014 for *Animale: The Curse of Goldilocks* (Gallimard). His most recent work is the science-fiction series *Phobos* (Robert Laffont).

Sarah Engell was born in Copenhagen, Denmark, on a snowy day in March 1979. Her educational and professional background is diverse, spanning from dream interpretation, pedagogy and psychiatry to performing and teaching dance, mentoring young adults with mental-health problems and baking waffles in The Tivoli Garden. But since gluing her first book together at the age of five, reading and writing has been her greatest passion. Engell published her first book in 2009 and is the author of nine books, including five YA titles. The novel *21 måder at dø* (*21 Ways to Die*), about cyberbullying and suicide, became a best-seller in Denmark and nominated for a prestigious award. Her latest novel *Hjertet er 1 organ* (*The Heart Is 1 Organ*) from 2016 is about self-harm and LGBT issues. Today Sarah Engell is a full time-writer and lives in Tårnby with her husband and two children.

Endre Lund Eriksen is one of Norway's most beloved children's and young-adult authors. His breakthrough came in 2002 with the book *Pitbull-Terje går amok*, which received excellent reviews and won him the 2002 Ministry of Culture's Prize for Best Children's Book. His young-adult books combine serious topics like bullying, anxiety, terrorism and prejudice with humour and suspense, in heartfelt stories like 'The Summer My Dad Turned Gay', 'Super' and 'There Is a Terrorist in My Bunk Bed'. He is also the author of the Dunderly series for smaller kids, several picture books and two novels for adults. His books are popular abroad and have been translated into eleven languages. He is also a screenwriter and a film producer, as well as the co-owner of Fabelfjord Animation Studio based in Tromsø.

Laura Gallego is a Spanish YA author, specializing mainly in fantasy. She studied Spanish Literature and Language Studies at the University of Valencia, and in 1999 she won the El Barco de Vapor Award with *Finis Mundi*, a novel set in the Middle Ages. Three years later she was granted this same award for *The Legend of the Wandering King*. She currently has thirty published works under her belt, mainly focused on young readers, and has sold more than one million copies in Spain alone, with translations in sixteen languages. Her most popular YA novels are: *The Tower Chronicles*, *All the Fairies in the Kingdom*, *Wings of Fire* and especially the *Memories of Idhún* trilogy. In 2011, Gallego received the Cervantes Chico Award for her entire body of work, and in 2012 her novel, *Where the Trees Sing* won the National Award for Children's and Young Adult Literature.

Nina Elisabeth Grøntvedt, from Trondheim, Norway, had her debut as an author in 2006, with the picture book *The Little Hero* (*Den lille helten*), and she has been a full-time author and illustrator of children's books since 2009. Her main hobby growing up was drawing, and after high school she took courses in drawing and painting and studied graphic design. In her twenties she spent six years in Southampton, England, from where she has a degree in illustration. She has also studied creative writing and children's and young-adult literature at the Norwegian Institute of Children's Literature. Her international break-through came with the novel *Hey, It's Me!* (*Hei, det er meg!*), a fictional diary translated into six languages. *Ingvar Lykke's Butt* (*Rumpa til Ingvar Lykke*) is her first teen novel, and her first book without illustrations.

Finn-Ole Heinrich was born in 1982 near Hamburg in Germany. Before study-ing film directing in Hanover, he completed his civilian service, which saw him reading the newspaper to a man every day for nine months. Heinrich debuted as an author at the age of twenty-three with the short-story collection *die taschen voll wasser* (*pockets full of water*, 2005). This was followed by Heinrich's first novel *Räuberhände* (*The Boy with the Robber's Hands*, 2007) and a second volume of stories, *Gestern war auch schon ein Tag* (*Yesterday Was Also a* Day, 2009). *Frerk, du Zwerg!* (*Frerk, You Dwarf!*, 2011) is Heinrich's first book for children, illustrated by the Icelandic-Norwegian illustrator Rán Flygenring. From 2013 to 2014 Heinrich released the *Maulina Schmitt* trilogy. He has received many awards, among these the Kranichsteiner Literaturförderpreis (2008) and the Deutscher Jugendliteraturpreis (German Youth Literature Prize 2012) and the LUCHS. He lives as a freelance author in Hamburg and France.

Michaela Holzinger grew up on a farm in Austria and was already composing stories on an invisible typewriter before she could actually write. Later she bought a laptop and her stories appeared as books. She lives with her family and a motley crew of goats and donkeys in a house in the woods. She has published almost twenty books for all ages, some of which have won awards.

Peder Frederik Jensen was born in 1978 in Copenhagen, Denmark, and attended the Danish School of Writers. He had his debut in 2007 with the novel *Her står du* (*You're Standing Here*). He is a trained boat-builder and has collaborated with other young authors for the Danish magazine for the homeless, *Hus forbi*. In 2009 he founded the literary magazine *Morgenrøde.dk* with three other authors. Peder Frederik Jensen received Albert Dams Mindelegat Prize in 2012, the Dramatic Debut Award in 2015 and the highly prestigious Otto Gelsted Prize in 2016.

Sanne Munk Jensen, born in Skagen in 1979, is a firmly established voice in Danish YA literature. Her acclaimed novel *Closest* debuted in 2002, and was followed by the breakthrough *One Day the Sun Shines Also on a Dog's Ass* (2007), which was a commercial success and earned her Gyldendal's Børnebogspris (Youth Literature) and the Orla Prize. *Satan's Brood* (2010) and *Arangutang* (2012) were also acclaimed by readers and critics alike. The YA novel *You and Me at Dawn* (2014), which Jensen co-authored with Glenn Ringtved, earned her the prestigious author prize from the Ministry of Culture for children and youth books. Aside from being an author, Sanne Munk Jensen is also a screenwriter and has written several films and TV shows for children. She is a mother of two and now lives in Vesterbro in Copenhagen.

Sandrine Kao, born in 1984 in the Paris region and of Taiwanese origins, is an author and illustrator for young people. After studying publishing at the University of Paris X and illustration at the École Supérieure d'Art d'Épinal (Vosges), she gained a master in children's literature at the University of Cergy-Pontoise; Sandrine Kao's first picture books were published in 2008 by Éditions Gecko. Her first novels were published by Éditions Syros under the Tempo label, a collection of realist and contemporary novels for age ten plus. She has also worked as an illustrator for Éditions Grasset Jeunesse and Utopique.

Inna Manakhova, born in 1986 in Orenburg, Russia, finished high school in 2003 and went on to study English and French Philology and Linguistics at Orenburg State Pedagogical University, graduating with a degree in Linguistics in 2008. While working as a translator, she wrote on the side, but had never attempted to publish any of her early poems and short stories before 2012, when she entered the Debut literary competition in the category "short fiction", and her story was included in the long list. Soon afterwards she entered the Sergey Mikhalkov literary competition with the short novel *Twelve Spectators* and won the children's choice award. This short novel was published in Russian in 2016.

Annette Münch, born in Oslo, Norway, loved writing and martial arts from a young age. When she was seventeen she got her black belt, and when she was nineteen she started working on her first novel, *Kaoskrigeren (The Chaos Warrior)*, which was published six years later and was awarded the Ministry of Culture's book prize for best first novel. After studying media at the University of Oslo and Hedmark College and working as a freelance journalist, at the age of twenty-three she got a job as an editor for teenage magazines at Egmont, before moving to the newspaper *Aftenposten* seven years later. Today she is a full-time writer. Among her latest books are *Jenteloven (The Girl Code*, 2009, awarded the Norwegian Bookseller Federation's Prize for children and young adult books), *The Ultimate Guide to Martial Arts* (2012) and *Badboy: Steroid* (2014, awarded the Brage Prize for best children and young adult books and the Østfoldungdommens Kritikkerpris).

Ana Pessoa, born in 1982, is a Portuguese writer and translator living in Brussels. She has published three books for young adults: *Mary John, Supergiant* (selected for the White Ravens Catalogue 2015) and *The Karate Girls' Red*

Notebook (winner of the Branquinho da Fonseca Prize 2011). Ana's books are also published in Brazil, Colombia and Mexico. In her free time she writes a blog (www.belgavista.blogspot.com) and eats Belgian chocolate. She is also a member of several writers' groups. Many of her stories won awards in Portugal and abroad (Jovens Criadores 2013, Portugal; Castello di Duino 2011, Italy; Sea of Words 2010, Spain).

Gideon Samson, born in The Hague in the Netherlands, studied Dutch Language and Culture and subsequently Film Studies, both at the University of Amsterdam. When he was twenty-two his first book *Niks zeggen!* (*Don't Say a Thing!*) was published. The jury of the Pencils (the annual prizes for the best children books) honoured the book with its "with flying colours" recommendation. Two years later Samson was the youngest ever winner of a Silver Pencil for his book *Ziek* (*Ill*). In 2013 he won the Pencil again for *Zwarte zwaan* (*Black Swan*) and two years later he and co-author Julius 't Hart won the Golden Frame, the annual prize for the best young-adult book of the year, for *Overspoeld* (*Flooded*). Samson lives with his girlfriend in the centre of Amsterdam. A couple of months a year he spends on a mountain in the south of Crete.

Salla Simukka, born in 1981, is the author of the international success *The Snow White Trilogy*, with rights sold in fifty-two countries. She has also worked as a translator from Swedish to Finnish, as a literary critic and as an editor at a literary magazine for young people, *LUKUfiilis*. She has also worked as one of the scriptwriters for the Finnish Broadcasting Company YLE's series *Uusi Päivä* (*New Day*). Salla Simukka has written several novels and one collection of short prose for young readers, and has translated adult fiction, children's books and plays. Her accolades include the Topelius Prize in 2013 and the Finland Prize in 2013. Her latest novel is a middle-grade fantasy book called *Sisarla* (*Sisterland*). Salla Simukka lives in Tampere, Finland, and her hobbies include jogging, knitting, drawing and baking.

Elisabeth Steinkellner was born in 1981 and grew up in Lower Austria. After school she studied Social Education and Cultural Anthropology in Vienna and worked with children and teenagers on the side. In her free time she was also involved in contemporary dance, acrobatics, photography and writing. Her first book for children was published in 2010 and since then there have been various publications from her for children, teenagers and adults. Her stories and poems have won several awards and have been translated into many languages. The author lives with her family in Baden near Vienna.

Cornelia Travnicek lives in Lower Austria. She studied Chinese and Computer Science at the University of Vienna and works part-time as a researcher in its Centre for Virtual Reality and Visualization. Her literary works have won numerous awards, including the State of Lower Austria Commendation Award for her debut novel *Chucks* (*Converse*, 2012) and the Kranichstein Youth Literature Grant awarded by the German Literature Fund. In 2012 she received the audience award at the Festival of German-Language Literature in Klagenfurt for an extract from her novel *Junge Hunde* (*Young Dogs*). She has also written articles for various newspapers, magazines and journals. An Austrian film adaptation of *Chucks* was released in 2015.

ABOUT THE TRANSLATORS

Dan Bellm has published four books of poetry, most recently *Deep Well* (2017). His translations include *Speaking in Song* by Mexican poet Pura López Colomé, *The Song of the Dead* by French poet Pierre Reverdy, and Laura Gallego García's novel, *The Legend of the Wandering King*. He teaches at Antioch University Los Angeles.

Anne Bruce, who lives on the Isle of Arran in Scotland, formerly worked in education and has a long-standing love of Scandinavia. She studied Norwegian and English at Glasgow University and has translated several novels by Jørn Lier Horst and Anne Holt as well as Merethe Lindstrøm's Nordic Prize winner.

Jane Bugaeva translates children's literature and poetry from the Russian. She lives in North Carolina with her husband and daughter.

Charlotte Collins studied English Literature and worked as an actor and radio journalist before becoming a literary translator. Her translations include novels by Robert Seethaler (*A Whole Life*, shortlisted for the 2016 Man Booker International Prize, and *The Tobacconist*), *The Eighth Life* by Nino Haratischwili and several plays for children.

Katy Derbyshire translates contemporary German writers, including Inka Parei, Clemens Meyer, Jan Brandt, Felicitas Hoppe and many others. She writes occasional criticism and essays in English and German. Katy co-hosts a monthly literary translation lab in Berlin and has taught translation in London, Leipzig, New York, New Delhi and Norwich.

David Colmer translates poetry, novels and children's literature, mainly from Dutch. He has won a number of prizes for his work, including the IMPAC Dublin Literary Award and the *Independent* Foreign Fiction Prize, both with novelist Gerbrand Bakker.

Alison Entrekin's translations include works by authors such as Adriana Lisboa, Paulo Lins, Cristovão Tezza, Clarice Lispector, Chico Buarque, Tatiana Salem Levy, Raphael Montes and Daniel Galera. Her work has been shortlisted for many awards and she is a three-time finalist in the NSW Premier's Translation Prize & PEN Medallion.

Paul Russell Garrett translates from Norwegian and Danish, with a particular interest in theatre. Years of collaboration with [Foreign Affairs], an international theatre company based in East London, now sees him heading their translation programme. Paul teaches Danish at the University of Westminster and serves on the committee of the Translators Association.

Daniel Hahn is a writer, editor and translator with forty-something books to his name. His translations include books for both adults and children, from Portuguese, Spanish and French. Other recent books include the new *Oxford Companion to Children's Literature*. He is also the editor of these Aarhus 39 volumes.

Rosie Hedger is a freelance translator from Norwegian into English. Her translation of Agnes Ravatn's *The Bird Tribunal* won an English PEN Translates Award in 2016, with the book selected for BBC Radio 4's *Book at Bedtime*. Having lived in Norway, Sweden and Denmark, Rosie is now based in the UK.

Dina Leifer is a freelance translator from French and Italian with a love of children's fiction. She worked in journalism and communications for many years, before rediscovering her passion for languages and literature when she took an MA in Translating Popular Culture at City University of London in 2015.

Siân Mackie is a translator from Edinburgh. She translates from Norwegian, Danish and Swedish. Her work spans numerous genres including literary fiction, thriller and drama, and she has also translated and co-translated literature for children and young adults. She is based in Southampton.

Tim Mohr has translated novels by Alina Bronsky, Wolfgang Herrndorf and Charlotte Roche, as well as Stefanie de Velasco's *Tiger Milk*. He has also collaborated on memoirs with Duff McKagan, Gil Scott-Heron and Paul Stanley.

His own writing has appeared in *The New York Times*, *Playboy* and *Inked*, among other publications. Prior to starting his writing career, Mohr made his living as a club DJ in Berlin.

Alice Tetley-Paul translates from German, Dutch and Luxembourgish into English. She recently completed an MA in Literary Translation at UEA in Norwich. She has worked as a translator and editor in Luxembourg and Norwich and now translates from her Northumberland-based office, which she shares with her wife and cat.

Rachel Ward translates from German and French to English. Her published translations include the Nea Fox crime series by Amelia Ellis, and books for young people such as *Traitor* by Gudrun Pausewang and *Red Rage* by Brigitte Blobel. She lives in Wymondham, near Norwich. She tweets as @FwdTranslations and can also be found at www.forwardtranslations.co.uk

Owen F. Witesman has translated more than forty Finnish books into English. His recent translations include seven novels in the Maria Kallio detective series by Leena Lehtolainen and the *As Red as Blood* trilogy by Salla Simukka. This year will see the publication of his translation of Simukka's *Sisterland* by Crown Books for Young Readers.

ABOUT THE ILLUSTRATORS

Peter Bailey was born in India and grew up in London. Since graduating from Brighton College of Art, he has illustrated books for both children and adults, by some of Britain's best-known authors, such as Philip Pullman and Alexander McCall Smith.

Barroux is an award-winning illustrator who was born in Paris and spent much of his childhood in North Africa, before attending art school in France. His work includes the critically acclaimed picture books *Where's the Elephant?*, *Where's the Starfish?* and the extraordinary graphic novel, *Line of Fire, Diary of an Unknown Soldier*. His most recent picture book, *Welcome*, was inspired by the plight of refugees.

Rotraut Susanne Berner is a multi-award-winning German illustrator and author. She illustrates books for adults and children, and her work is loved all around the globe. In 2016 she was honoured with the prestigious Hans Christian Andersen award. Susanne is also a curator for the German Foundation of Illustration. She grew up in the countryside and now lives in Munich.

Serge Bloch is an award-winning French *dessinateur*. He illustrates for children's books, newspapers and advertising. He has been drawing for over thirty years, and loves it more with each passing day.

Kitty Crowther, who is half English and half Swedish, was born in Brussels and lives in Wallonia in Belgium. She's written and/or illustrated about forty books, which have been translated into twenty languages. In 2010, Kitty won the world's most prestigious prize for children's literature, the Astrid Lindgren Memorial Award.

Isol is an illustrator, cartoonist, graphic artist, writer, singer and composer from Argentina. She has published many books, which have been translated in many countries. In 2013, Isol won the prestigious Astrid Lindgren Memorial Award.

Joëlle Jolivet is a French illustrator and painter. She studied graphic design and advertising and attended the lithography workshop of the Beaux Arts in Paris. Her strong interest in engraving led her to lino-cutting, her main medium. Her children's books have been translated all over the world and have won many prizes.

Søren Jessen started out as an illustrator, but soon came to writing his own stories, anything from picture books all the way to YA. He still illustrates his and other authors' works. Søren has won many awards for his work. Born in Sønderborg, Denmark, he now lives in Aarhus.

Satoshi Kitamura's books have won many prizes, including the Mother Goose Award (for *Angry Arthur*) and the Smarties Prize (for *Me and My Cat*). After many years leaving in the UK, Satoshi is now back in his native Japan, where he studies Spanish in his spare time.

Ole Könnecke is a writer and illustrator whose award-winning picture books, comics and novels have been translated into many languages. He spent his childhood in Sweden and now lives in Hamburg, Germany.

Anke Kuhl studied Fine Arts in Mainz and Offenbach, Germany, and works as an illustrator and author since 1998. She lives in Frankfurt and is part of the LABOR studio collective. Her books have been awarded many times. She was awarded the prestigious German Jugendliteraturpreis for her book *Alles Familie*.

Yvonne Kuschel is a painter, illustrator, book designer and author. She has received many prizes and accolades and has taught drawing at the Hamburg Akademie der Wissenschaffen and the Leipzig Hochschule für Grafik and Buchkunst. She was born in Gdansk, Poland, and now lives in Leipzig with her family.

Hanne Kvist is a Danish writer and illustrator. She has received several literary awards for her work, including the nomination for the Nordic Council Children and Young People's Literature Prize 2014 and the Ministry of Culture's children book prize 2016.

Dave McKean has created many award-winning books and graphic novels, including *Cages* and *Black Dog: The Dreams of Paul Nash* and collaborations with Richard Dawkins, Ray Bradbury, Heston Blumenthal, John Cale, David Almond and Neil Gaiman. Dave is currently directing a fourth feature film, *Wolf's Child*, and creating a new graphic novel called *Caligaro*.

Jörg Mühle was born, lives and works in Frankfurt am Main in Germany. He studied illustration in Offenbach and Paris and has been illustrating for books and magazines since 2000. His board book *Tickle My Ears* has become an international best-seller. Jörg is part of the LABOR studio collective.

Ella Okstad lives in Norway, with her husband, three children and a cat. Since graduating from the Kent Institute of Art and Design in 2000, Ella has worked with well-known publishers in Norway, the UK and the US. She illustrates the *Squishy McFluff* series written by Pip Jones, which has been an international success.

Mårdøn Smet is an award-wining Danish cartoonist who has been illustrating for over three decades. His work is eclectic: he illustrates comics – alternative and mainstream – as well as children's classics and contemporary horror and fairy tales.

Helen Stephens is a multi-award-winning English author-illustrator. She is known for her line work and bright, instantly recognizable illustrations, loved by children big and small. She has also collaborated with acclaimed authors such as Michael Morpurgo and Roger McGough.

Britta Teckentrup is an award-winning illustrator, author and fine artist. She was born in Hamburg and studied illustration and fine art at St Martin's College and the Royal College of Art in London. Britta has published over ninety books in over twenty countries. She lives in Berlin with her husband, their son Vincent and their cat Oskar.

ABOUT THE AARHUS 39

Aarhus 39 is a collection of the best emerging writers for young people from across wider Europe. The authors have been selected by three of Europe's much-loved writers – Kim Fupz Aakeson (Denmark), Ana Cristina Herreros (Spain) and Matt Haig (UK) – and commissioned to write an original story to the theme of 'Journey'.

The writers are invited to spend five days in Aarhus visiting schools and taking part in the International Children's Literature Hay Festival in Aarhus which runs 26–29th October 2017.

The 39 selected writers are:

1. Ævar Þór Benediktsson – Iceland
2. Alaine Agirre – Spain
3. Aline Sax – Belgium
4. Ana Pessoa – Portugal
5. Andri Antoniou – Cyprus
6. Anna Woltz – Netherlands
7. Annelise Heurtier – France
8. Annette Münch – Norway
9. B.R. Collins – UK
10. Cathy Clement – Luxembourg
11. Cornelia Travnicek – Austria
12. David Machado – Portugal
13. Dy Plambeck – Denmark
14. Elisabeth Steinkellner – Austria
15. Endre Lund Eriksen – Norway
16. Finn-Ole Heinrich – Germany
17. Frida Nilsson – Sweden
18. Gideon Samson – Netherlands
19. Inna Manakhova – Russia

20. Jana Šrámková – Czech Republic
21. Katherine Rundell – UK
22. Katherine Woodfine – UK
23. Laura Dockrill – UK
24. Laura Gallego – Spain
25. Ludovic Flamant – Belgium
26. Maria Parr – Norway
27. Maria Turtschaninoff – Finland
28. Michaela Holzinger – Austria
29. Nataly Elisabeth Savina – Germany
30. Nina Elisabeth Grøntvedt – Norway
31. Peder Frederik Jensen – Denmark
32. Salla Simukka – Finland
33. Sandrine Kao – France
34. Sanne Munk Jensen – Denmark
35. Sarah Crossan – Ireland
36. Sarah Engell – Denmark
37. Stefan Bachmann – Switzerland
38. Stefanie de Velasco – Germany
39. Victor Dixen – France

For more information, please visit
www.hayfestival.com/aarhus39

COPYRIGHT INFORMATION